Chasing Cthulhu

Urf Oomons Book Two

Bebe Harper

Gratefully dedicated to Carol, Charlene, Crystal, and Rena

CHAPTER ONE

—GLORIA—

There is a giant, unknown sea-creature hiding right under my kayak. At first, I thought it was a giant Pacific octopus. That would have been incredible because I'm observing it in a cove in the Florida Keys. This is obviously Atlantic waters and there shouldn't be a giant Pacific octopus here. It blends in very well with its surroundings. But I get the feeling like I'm being watched. You know, that prickly, goosebumps feeling?

Looking over the side of my kayak, I see it. My dog, Princess Peach, sees it too, and starts yapping her little furry head off. It has long tentacles like an octopus, but it's kind of burrowed and balled up. I've passed over it a few times since first seeing it and can't quite envision what its whole body looks like. But it has claws, and those claws are on the end of fingers, I swear to God! And once I saw a mouth full of teeth. I probably don't have to tell you that's weird for an octopus.

This time, I've strapped a waterproof camera to the underside of my kayak. Now I'm taking a video of this octopus-creature-animal. As unlikely as it seems, I believe I've discovered a new species. I need to Google how to go about this. I think I get to name it if I discover it, right?

My first instinct is to name it something funny, but when I think about it, I'm not actually any good at coming up with funny names. And I haven't really gotten a good look at it. It's so well camouflaged that I only ever see one part or another and not the thing as a whole. Maybe after I look at this video, I'll be able to come up with a good name for this newly discovered species.

I'm startled out of my thoughts when Peach starts barking again. But this time she's barking toward the house and not the tentacled creature on the seafloor. There's a truck pulling down the long driveway of my very private vacation rental.

I'm instantly terrified, but I give myself a pep-talk. I'm sure it's not what I think it is. Not everybody is out to get me. They're probably lost.

I consider just paddling away. If I turn left out of this cove, I can paddle right over to the nearby restaurant and get out at their dock.

And then what?

I don't even have my phone with me. I left it inside like a dumb ass because I didn't want to be interrupted by notifications. Social media has become a danger to me in real life. It's better to stay away from it as much as possible right now. I could paddle over to the restaurant and ask to use their phone, maybe? And then call the police or something? I stop considering this ridiculous scenario. The cops would laugh at me. It's just a truck in the driveway. They aren't breaking any laws. Plus, the restaurant hostess wouldn't let me past the door with my dog in tow.

So that settles it. I can't paddle away from this truck. I can wait it out though. Just stay out here on the water until they leave.

They shut off the ignition and step down out of the truck. There are two guys in jeans, T-shirts, and neck-gators. You know the kind of mask that is a piece of fabric that goes around your whole neck? That's not too weird with the pandemic and everything, but it feels creepy.

They knock on the door. When no one answers, they hang around, leaning against the truck. One turns his head to look out at the cove, then sees me. He elbows his friend and they both walk over to the dock.

I don't know what to do.

I've had a lot of bad experiences lately with strange men. I know I shouldn't let it cloud my judgement and turn me into one of those women who hate *all* men. But I'm getting such a bad vibe.

The whole point of this trip is to relax, away from people. Avoid attention, stay off social media, just let it all go and completely unwind.

I've splurged on this vacation. I've spent so much that I hadn't planned to. Not just on the rental, but also new swimwear, a kayak, a GoPro, life vests for me and my dog, and on and on.

I have been able to relax for once.

But here are these guys, coming up the driveway, waving and yelling at me.

"Hey, you!"

I paddle a little closer so I can hear them. "Can I help you?"

"This your car?"

I just look at them for a second, confused. What do they care about my rental car?

"Yeah, it's mine."

He looks angry about my answer. "Well, you need to get it out of here. We rented this place for the weekend and there's not supposed to be anyone here."

"No way," I argue. "I'm paid up here for a month. You need to check the address again because you got the wrong place."

"We don't have the wrong place, you've probably overstayed —"

Then I can't hear anything else he says because Peach starts yapping her furry ass off. Ugh, this is so annoying. I better not have to leave. I was just getting into the groove here. And what about the octopus-animal I've discovered? I'm going to be pissed if the owner has double booked and messed me up.

Paddling over to the dock, I haul myself out of the kayak, scoop up my pup, and walk toward the cottage. "I'll just give the owner a call and see what's up."

And that's when they grab me.

CHAPTER TWO

—LU—

Something is terribly wrong. I think my human has been attacked. It is hard to tell from my vantage point. Usually I try to remain hidden as I watch her, but now I have floated up from the seafloor to spy on them. I am still too far away to know the details of what is happening. Perhaps it is Earth-Human mating behavior? Many species engage in courting rituals that would seem violent to an ignorant observer. I do not like it, but if this is consensual then I need not concern myself. But the way she is hanging limply in their grasp, and the pungent medicinal odor hanging on the breeze—this does not feel right.

Drifting closer to the dock, I move nearer to the surface, so my head is out of the water. Now I can hear that noisy little animal of hers screeching and snarling in its high-toned way as it bounds around their feet. And now one of the males kicks out with his lower limb and strikes the animal! This cannot be right. She would never allow her animal companion to be damaged. Obviously, these miscreants are not breeding partners, they are predators that mean her harm.

Without making a conscious decision to do so, I surge up to the rocky shore, next to the dock. They are wrestling her limp form into their land vehicle, and I must hurry, or they could drive off. They can't escape. How would I track her then? How would I save her from this attack?

I am not a violent male. I have never struck another being

in anger and I always work to find peaceful solutions to conflict. All that is forgotten now. They have harmed this delicate little female. My female. The thought of mercy does not occur to me. After silently sneaking up on them, my tentacles working quickly to get there before they can close the door. They have carelessly tossed her in the rear seating area of their conveyance. I grab both males in my tentacles and squeeze the very breath out of them before they can protest. I hear their bones snapping and grinding together as I apply more force, then lift them both high into the air and bash them together. I have surely killed them, but I bash them together one more time to make sure. I heave and toss them as far as I can out into the ocean. I hear a distant splash and hope that one of those great sharp-toothed sea predators disposes of them so that my female does not have to see their corpses wash ashore. Perhaps it would have been better to weigh them down somehow.

Stilling for a moment now that the threat is gone, I take a deep breath and relax my tentacles. I look around, making sure there are no humans who might have witnessed my violent, murderous outburst. There are none. I feel calm. Should I not be dismayed, having just murdered two beings? Soft little human males no less? This was not fair combat. I try to think it over and I feel justified. These males deserve no mercy, no consideration.

I should leave though.

In the conveyance that those males arrived in, my female is still unconscious, thrown over a lumpy seat she looks very uncomfortable. Looking around, I see a length of fabric stretched between two trees and attached with some rope. I have seen her recline there before. That would be a much better place to rest her form until she wakes from this drugged sleep. I carefully move her out and over to the fabric. As I carry her in my upper arms, her weight is warm and lush. Her mane is soft and fragrant, and holding her close is a pleasure. I am tempted to hold her until she wakes.

No. That is a terrible idea.

I deposit her gently in the tree-sling and then I go find her animal. It is alive, but unconscious as well and seems to have a contusion on its brow. And another by its ear. Poor little beast. I place it on top of its human.

It is then that I notice I'm covered in bright red blood. I have gotten quite a bit of it on the human when I carried her. It's all in her hair. It's covering my tentacles and upper torso. How did that happen? I must have squeezed the lifeblood right out of those males. Gross.

A swim is obviously in order. But I feel like should do more to ensure the comfort of my human. Will she feel alone and disoriented when she awakens? I should maybe stay and comfort her. No. That would terrify her. I must keep squashing this impulse to reveal myself to her. It would serve no purpose at all and only upset her. Especially since I am coated in the blood of her enemies. I recall that my podmate's human was so easily startled. No, I cannot allow her to see me. But neither can I let her out of my sight until she awakens. What if those males I disposed of are not the only ones who mean her harm? What if more come and she is not even awake to defend herself?

I waffle, not knowing the right course of action. I need to be near, but hidden. There is a copse of trees on the other side of the outdoor pool. I decide to duck into the shade there and camouflage.

CHAPTER THREE
—GLORIA—

Peach is barking like crazy at something. As usual. But I have such a terrible headache right now, I wish she would stop.

"Peach!" I try to yell at her, but it comes out as a scratchy croak and talking hurts my head more.

I go to get up so I can get her, but the bed moves, and I flip over out of it, hitting my hip and elbow on...gravel? Why am I out by the driveway?

Must've fallen asleep in the hammock. Groggily, I look around.

No.

There's that truck those two guys drove up in. They grabbed me and—I don't know. But the inside of my mouth feels all dry and tastes like someone shoved a ball of cotton candy in there and then dissolved it with hand sanitizer. Gross.

Something happened. Those guys did something, but I can't remember. And where the hell are they? Their truck is right there. Why knock me out just to leave me here in this hammock?

This is a new level to the harassment I've had to deal with this past year. There's been threatening emails, phone calls, doxing (that's when someone finds your personal information like address, phone number, legal name and make it public) and swatting. The swatting was particularly bad. It's a kind of prank where someone calls in an anonymous tip to have a swat team bust into your home in full gear. This is the first time these Men's

Rights guys have actually shown up and harmed me.

What can I do about this? Is there some place I could move to be safe from them? Do I have to hire bodyguards?

And what the hell is Peach barking at?

She's probably harassing some poor squirrel or something. I swear that dog causes no end of trouble.

Squinting and shading my eyes because the sun is exacerbating my headache, I shuffle carefully over to my pup. I'm all woozy, obviously an aftereffect of whatever those assholes used to knock me out. I keep listing a little to the side and tripping over my own feet, but I finally make it over to Peach and—

Hole. Eee. Shit.

There is something a lot bigger than a squirrel and Peach is attacking it, biting the heck out of it, and snarling and just being so very dumb. That thing that she has a hold of is huge and monstrous. My brain won't even deal with it, it's that terrifying. I want to run, but I can't just leave Peach.

The creature is backing up and kind of shrinking away from me. It's hard to keep track of it because the color of its skin keeps changing. It blends in well with its camouflage, but not perfectly. It's trying to disappear even as it shrinks away but Peach has no trouble keeping ahold of it. For a terrible Lovecraftian horror, it's acting scared. But Peach follows and she has bitten it so hard that she's drawing blood and the blood is a blue-purple. Slowly, the giant beast lifts a leg—no, a tentacle—up into the air and Peach is hanging from it, still biting and snarling. It extends the tentacle and my dog forward until I can reach over and snatch her away.

That's when I see that Peach is hurt. She has a big cut over her eye and her fur is all matted with blood and sand.

"What did you do to my dog?" I yell at the monster, my anger making me just as dumb as Peach, "she's just a little dog, you big jerk."

The thing continues moving away from me, holding up human-like hands with long black talons. Its eyes big and yellow with vertical slits are wide in alarm.

"You get the hell out of here!" I yell some more, waving an arm at it and stomping my foot. And it does. It starts backing up, creeping toward the shore. Now that I can see it in the light, it is the strangest thing.

Okay, picture Ursula from the Little Mermaid, with an octopus bottom and human top, but all gray, with a bald head and ruffled ears. Also huge, not curvaceous like Ursula, but strong-looking. Like Ursula's giant, bald, fit cousin. With long-ass claws on its fingers and a kind of flat bump for a nose. And yellow eyes with vertically slit pupils.

So weird.

As it slips into the water, I recall the sea creature I had been trying to get a video of. It was this thing! The whole time I was kayaking in that cove there was a giant tentacle monster lurking under there, concealing itself so well that I couldn't tell what it looked like at all.

I stand there staring at the water where the monster has just disappeared. The water is calm, with no ripples at all. Nothing to give away that that enormous terrifying creature is below the surface.

This has been the weirdest frickin day of my life.

CHAPTER FOUR

—GLORIA—

It's been three days since the incident, and I haven't seen the tentacle monster. If I didn't have videos and photos from when I was trying to document it as a new species, I would think that I had imagined it all. But I do have the videos and photos. I keep reviewing them over and over. Now that I know what I'm looking at, because I've seen it in the light of day, it's easy to make sense of the thing. The video is good, but it really doesn't give the whole picture.

This is just amazing. I'm tempted to load a short video up on Tik-Tok just to ask people what they think. Am I going crazy, or will they see this, too?

But, of course, I'm not going to do that. I could just picture this creature going viral and tons of people looking for it. It would be like the Bigfoot of the ocean. And what if someone did find it? They wouldn't just leave it alone, they would try to catch it.

And social media is what got me into my current situation. There is no reason on this earth for me to log back on.

I close my laptop and look out the window facing the driveway. That big truck is still there. I still have no idea what happened to those guys and no, I have not reported the incident to the police. First, what exactly am I going to say? "These two guys grabbed me and knocked me out somehow, then they disappeared, and I woke up to find my dog attacking a tentacle monster, who I shooed back into the ocean." Secondly, my experiences with reporting stuff to the police have been very negative so far. At best, they've been totally useless, at worst, they low-key blame me for whatever is going on.

I do contact the owner of this rental to have that truck towed, though. Just so I don't have to keep seeing it.

When the tow comes, the guy sees me lounging by the pool and comes over to ask, "This your truck?"

"No, I don't know whose it is." One hundred percent true.

"Ok, well, I've been asked to tow it by the property owner," he explains like I might object.

"Good. Thanks," I reply. I look up at him from my book. He looks exactly like you might expect a tow truck driver to look. White guy with a dadbod, sunglasses, scraggly brown hair, T-shirt, jeans, and scuffed work boots.

This guy isn't making me uncomfortable at all and it's a stark contrast to how I was immediately creeped out by those other two guys even before they got out of their truck. Maybe I have better intuition than I thought, and I should trust it from now on.

He starts to head back toward his tow truck, but then he stops and comes back over to me to ask, "Have you seen anything weird lately?"

"Huh?" I ask. How does he know?

"There's been a few UFO sightings in the area, you know? Like legit ones, in the news and everything." He looks a bit embarrassed asking about it.

"UFOs," I repeat slowly. "No, I haven't seen anything like that."

He shrugs. "Well, you should keep a look out," he tells me then turns back to his truck. "This place is smack dab in the middle of all of it."

As the guy is pulling the pickup onto the bed of the tow truck, I pull out my phone. I had all the notifications turned off so I could relax on this vacation. Even after everything that's happened, I'm still trying to stick to that rule. No social media, no news, nothing like that. But I turn it on and search "UFO Florida Keys" and sure enough, the tow truck guy is right. There have been a whole lot of sightings of flying saucer-looking things. Back when the pandemic first started there were a few news articles about UFOs being sighted and government agencies corroborating it, but I wasn't really paying attention to all that. I guess UFOs, aliens, and stuff like that are real things now, not just conspiracy stuff.

Huh. Aliens.

So, it could be that the tentacle monster isn't really an undiscovered species that just happened to make its home in this cove. It would make a lot more sense that it is an alien somehow connected to these UFOs.

I would like to get another look at it because it did look more like a monstrous person than an animal. Its head and upper torso looked very human-ish.

I glance over to where the driver is strapping the pickup onto the flatbed of his tow truck, and I see something move behind him on the dock. I squint and shade my eyes to see better and it's a bald man coming out of the water.

No, not a man. It's the tentacle monster/alien. It's bobbing in the water, then grabbing onto the dock. The tow truck guy isn't facing the right way, but there's a real possibility that he's going to turn and see this monstrous thing coming out of the water.

And then what will happen?

My heart rate picks up and I tense with worry. Will the guy scream? Call the police or the news?

I don't know what I want to happen. This has had me stymied for the past few days. I can't come to a decision about this tentacle monster situation and if this guy sees it, then it's out of my hands, isn't it?

It has pulled itself out of the water and is coming up onto the rocky shore by the dock. I'm suddenly glad that I left Peach in her crate inside. Otherwise, she would be barking up a storm and drawing attention to the creature.

"Ma'am?"

I startle because the tow truck guy has snuck up on me.

"Yeah?" I ask dumbly.

"Here's my card in case they come looking for their truck." With that, he hands me a business card.

"Oh, ok. Thanks." I take the card.

"You take care now." He tips his hat and I nod back.

The tentacle monster is just standing there on the dock, and I can see that all of its tentacles are kind of moving around even though the top part is standing still. I'm sure the tow truck guy is going to turn and see it.

He doesn't, he hops right into his tow truck and drives off. Must not have looked back once because the tentacle monster is right-frickin-there. And now I'm alone with it. This was not great planning on my part. I should have said something, kept that guy from driving off.

What do I do now?

I just stand here by the pool, staring through the fence at it for a full minute. It doesn't come any closer.

Lifting my phone, I start snapping pictures. Then I switch to video.

It waves at me. I swear to God. He moves his hand through the air in a wave just like a human person would do.

This is amazing.

I wave back, holding the phone steady, and yell, "Hello!"

It responds but in a kind of bubbly hiccup sound. Huh, maybe some sort of alien language?

"Can you understand me?" I ask carefully.

It nods, but not very naturally. Its chin moves down too far then up too high, like an exaggerated mimicry of a nod.

Unlatching the gate, I step through, a few feet closer to it.

"Are you an alien?"

Another careful nod.

Wow. Well, that settles that. Here I am making contact with an honest-to-goodness alien. I wonder if anyone will ever believe this? But I suddenly recall Peach and the cut above her eye, and I ask angrily, "Why did you hurt my dog?"

It holds dangerously clawed hands up and I step back behind the fence, but it's shaking its head back and forth, this gesture more natural than the nodding. It's burbling in its alien language and its whole demeanor is one of denial.

"You didn't hurt Peach?"

Careful nod.

"Then who did?"

It waves toward where that pickup truck had been parked.

"The two men who came in that truck?"

Another nod.

"And what happened with them?"

Burbling emphatically, the alien waves its clawed hands. Its skin, previously a dull gray is darkening to black. Around its neck, there is a red splotch that's spreading across its shoulders. Two tentacles wave up in front of its torso and then slap together once, twice, then make a hurling motion toward the other side of the property where the back yard faces the open ocean.

Holy shit. "You did that?"

A nod. Its color is washing out, returning to shark-gray.

"Are they dead then?"

Emphatic nod.

I glance down at the phone. It's still pointed at the alien, still recording. I can't believe I now have a recording of an alien confessing to murder. This is wild.

"Why would you kill them?" I ask breathlessly.

Burbling sounds.

It makes a beseeching gesture toward me and a couple tentacles wave toward where the truck had been, then more burbling sounds.

So, I guess this giant, terrifying alien was protecting me? What am I supposed to do with that? I sure as heck didn't ask it to murder anyone.

"Um." I think hard for an appropriate response because I don't want to offend this violent alien. "Thanks?"

CHAPTER FIVE

—LU—

"Thanks." The female says in her Earth-Human speak. The language is just as adorable as humans themselves, all chirps, and squeaks.

This is a strange culture that these Earth-Humans have. Apparently, it is a regular thing for males to just show up at a female's residence, maybe to assault her and abduct her, or maybe not. And how am I to know when this human female is in danger or not? Which males are predatory, and which are benign?

When I heard another vehicle coming up to my human's house, I was ready to do violence again to protect her, but it was unnecessary because this human male meant no harm at all. There was not a whiff of anxiety in the air, and the male was relaxed. Keeping close to be sure of the female's safety, I watched as the two interacted. The only thing he did was speak to my female and then leave, taking the criminals' vehicle with him.

I am still shocked at myself. Did I really kill two people? Even as I ponder it, I am willing to do so again. Is this just who I am now? A violent, obsessed male?

My introspection yields no answers, and it is not clear what she is thankful for now. That I killed those first two men? Or that I did not kill her most recent visitor? Could be that she is thankful that it was not I who harmed her small animal companion.

She is trying to communicate with me, and it is so charming. I obviously have the advantage in our conversation thanks to my universal translation implant. It was updated with Earth-Human speak a while ago. I cannot speak it though because my people, Homeworlders, vocalize in an entirely different way than these humans and cannot physically make the Earth-Speak sounds. I doubt she can make Homeworlder sounds. She is so very focused on understanding me, though. Her brows with their tiny lines of fur are drawn together in concentration. She is even taking a video for later study.

My admiration for this little female grows as she remains in my presence, working to communicate with me. What a different creature she is from the human female my pod-mate brought on our ship so long ago. Tiny quaked in terror and passed out in fear when she first got a good look at me, but this one is so brave and fierce. Not only did she berate me, stomping her delicate foot at me when she thought I had harmed her animal, now here she stands questioning me as though not concerned at all. It is too much.

As if by their own will, my tentacles have been moving me incrementally closer as we converse. She gives no sign of noticing.

"Are those *Yew-Eff-Ohs* searching for you?"

I shrug my tentacles in confusion. That word is not in the translation matrix.

She stabs a digit at her device. Poke, poke, poking it with her nimble little finger. Is there anything she does that is not absolutely adorable?

Turning the screen toward me, she slowly moves through a collection of images. I move the last little distance closer to her so that I may see them clearly. They are almost all Seereechee drone vessels.

Alarmed, I jerk back from the device and look around us, searching the sky. But it is fast becoming overcast with clouds, and I see nothing. The atmosphere on this planet is so changeable. One moment the single star Earth orbits shines down hotly and the next a cloud of dense, moist air blocks it and everything cools. One day everything is calm, the next there are great gusts of wind and pounding rains. It is a wonder.

"You recognize them?" She draws my attention from the clouded sky.

I perform a human nod of agreement.

"Are they looking for you?"

I nod again and I can feel my color darkening with thoughts of Seereechee drones searching for me. This has been a constant pressure, weighing me down. I do not even know how they are managing to get people from the surface of this planet up to their ship. And for that matter, how did I end up imprisoned on their ship? I had been dining in the cafeteria of our homeship, I must have lost consciousness because I woke up months later imprisoned on a Seereechee ship.

I should not be out in the open here conversing with her. My working theory has been that the Seereechees have not picked me up again because the water interferes with their tracking in some way. Every moment I am out in the air is a chance that they will find me, but I cannot stop moving toward her instead of away.

"You don't look happy about it. You don't want them to find you?"

My head swivels from side to side in negation.

"Huh. Well, I guess that's why you're hiding out here."

No, I am hiding out here to stay close to her and watch her so that I can intercede if she is attacked again by any more of these Earth-Human males. There is a whole world of oceans I could be moving through, staying ahead of Seereechee detection, but I cannot bring myself to leave her unguarded. What would have happened had I not been here to defend her earlier?

"So," she draws my attention back, "If that's a 'no' then why are you hiding out here?"

"To keep you safe," I explain, gesturing toward her with one hand and two tentacles. She does not understand. Without a device to access the translation matrix, all she hears when I speak is the incomprehensible vocalizations of Homeworlder speech. She does seem to pick up on the meaning of my gestures though because her eyes widen a tick. She lifts a hand to point at herself with one delicate digit, and she takes one step back. She is acting as though I have said something threatening when I have not.

To communicate that I mean no harm. I hold my hand up, palms out in a universal gesture of peace, move back a pace, and hold still.

That is when I see it.

Directly over her home, unveiling itself from dense cloud cover as it lowers, is a Seereechee drone shuttle. Silent and ominous, this disk-shaped spacecraft has not even caught her attention, though it is almost overhead.

My first instinct is to grab her and carry us both to the safety of the water. I could swim miles away from here. But of course, I cannot do that. Humans are unable to breathe underwater and cannot hold their breath for more than a few moments.

The only option is her domicile.

I reach out arms and tentacles, grab her up and move quickly toward the house. She yells in fright, scenting of alarm and fear. Her distress only grows when she catches sight of the ship.

The mechanism for the doorway is some barbaric puzzle that I do not take the time to figure out. I just bust through, causing glass and wood splinters to fly. I cover my human's delicate face as a few shards bounce off the wall and back toward us.

To one side of the door is a room with an over-abundance of windows and to the other side is a corridor. I take the corridor because the more concealed we are from that shuttle, the better.

On either side of this corridor, there are doors, but they are closed with the same puzzling mechanism, a knobby perturbance that does absolutely nothing when I press on it. At the end is an open door. I make my way there with this human yelling incoherently the whole time.

When I push the door the rest of the way open, I enter a strange room and rush across to flatten myself and my female on the other side of a—well, it is a large soft surface. It scents strongly of the human, more so than the rest of this home. Is this where she sleeps? No matter, the only concern right now is hiding. Can I even hide from the Seereechees when they can track my implant? I cannot remember how they got me the first time. How can I protect us from them?

There is a hard case next to us. It is barking. No, of course it's not barking, the animal locked within it is barking. I jam the end of a tentacle into the case and the barking little beast quiets because now he is chewing on my appendage. That is fine so long as he quiets.

"Why!?" The human starts yelling, "What is going on? You—umphh."

I have wrapped a tentacle around her face, silencing her mouth. She bites me and I allow it. There is no way to know if this noisy Earther could draw the Seereechees to us.

Now I crouch and wait, being chewed on by two ridiculous earth creatures and hunted by a slaving pirate species, and hope for luck. Maybe they will give up the chase. Maybe they did not notice us at all.

But fortune is not with me this day. A blue light shines through the fabric-covered window across the room and when that strange light falls on me, I am suddenly limp. My tentacles fall away from the beings I had been holding securely, my body rises weightlessly from the floor, and I pass into unconsciousness.

CHAPTER SIX

—GLORIA—

Okay. I've now officially been abducted by aliens. Not the tentacled kind like the one that had been hiding out in the cove, but the gray kind with big heads and flat-black oval-shaped eyes. The kind of aliens that you see in memes and on cartoons. Let me tell you they're a lot creepier in real life.

Peach and I had woken up in a clear cage. The walls of this cage are so clear, light doesn't reflect or refract as it would through glass, so you can't see them at all. I only know about the cage walls because I've bumped into every one of them. I've also tripped across a mess of limp tentacles that are strewn over the floor because the tentacle alien is imprisoned with me.

I don't have a stitch of clothing. Peach is missing her collar, harness, and bow. The tentacle monster/alien is just as naked and weird looking as ever lying passed out on the floor. Whatever those gray aliens did to knock us out seems to have worked twice as well on him.

There is something not right about this room. I mean, besides the aliens and invisible walls. It's like a giant warehouse, but it's foggy. Not real fog, but I can't see anything at a distance. My eyesight is failing me at a couple meters outside this cage. Any distance farther than that is an indecipherable blur. The gray aliens keep moving in and out of this unnatural field. It gives a very disturbing effect that this cage is standing alone in the middle of a vast and empty room. I don't know if the grays with their disappearing/reappearing act makes it more creepy or less creepy.

When the tentacle alien saw all those pictures of flying saucers, he looked worried. And then when he saw that one in the sky, he freaked the hell out, snatched me up into his arms and tentacles, and then tried to hide. I guess all this means is that these gray aliens are bad news. They aren't doing anything though. They just come up to the invisible wall and look at us. Sometimes point an oval tablet-looking thing at us, and then leave without a sound.

"Hello?" A disembodied, feminine voice sounds behind me. I scramble over the pile of tentacles to the other side of our cage.

"Hello!" I yell back. I peer and squint as hard as I can, but I can't see her.

"Oh, thank god! Do you know what's going on? Where are we?"

"On a spaceship, I think." I feel dumb saying it, but it's the truth.

"What?"

The question is a gasp. A few snickers sound from another direction.

Another voice from off to the side says, "Shut-up girls and maybe we can get out of time-out."

This command leads to a whole lot of commentary from all sides.

"Like I care!"

"Like I want to see your face anyway!"

"I like time-out."

"Fuck off!"

"Go fuck yourself, Karen!"

"W-what is time out?" the first voice asks.

"It's the fog. Whenever we get too rowdy, this fog appears so we can't see each other." Karen replies. That might not be her name, maybe she just acts like a Karen.

"It's on a timer. It doesn't matter if we talk or not," a new voice says with an air of reason.

"Yeah, but they probably start the timer over when we talk too much," says Karen.

"They never have," replies the voice of reason. "It's always around twenty minutes, no matter whether we talk or not."

"How many people are here? All women?" I ask.

"Eighteen," Karen answers.

"Twenty with you two new girls, and yes, all women," the voice of reason corrects.

"What about aliens?" I ask.

There's silence after I ask that, then, "What do you mean? The grays?"

"No, besides them. Are there any other aliens in cages? Ones with tentacles?"

More silence.

"No," a new voice says tentatively. "But there's a spider alien."

Spider alien?

The fog is lifting. One second it's there, the next it's gone and I can see all the other women. They are just standing, everybody is staggered a couple meters apart. And they're all by themselves in their own cages. Except I can see, behind everybody else, up against a far wall, a giant spider hovering over a prone human woman. I can't see any details about this spider, but it is enormous, black, with eight long, spidery legs. Comparing its size to the woman's, I would guess it's more than ten feet tall.

"What the hell is that an octopus?" At first, I didn't realize what Karen was talking about. It's a giant spider, not an octopus —

Then I look at her, tearing my gaze away from the monstrous spider, and see that she's pointing into my cage. Oh yeah, there is a giant octopus in here. Sort of.

"It's an alien," I answer primly.

"Why do you have an alien?" she asks like that is a reasonable question that I could answer.

I don't answer her. I just take in her look. She is naked like the rest of us here, and there's nothing wrong with her body. She has the soft, curvy form of a middle-aged woman. She has one of those soccer-mom haircuts. Short in the back and longer in the front, her light brown-to-dark blonde do is parted to one side and meticulously styled. There are highlights and lowlights, all obvious and chunky.

While I'm checking her out, she's looking right back at me from about fifteen feet away. Her eyes suddenly get big, and she says, "You have a dog?"

I don't know what she's accusing me of. Maybe this screechy, blame-full tone is just her default. I'm done talking with her though. I turn away so I'm not even looking at her.

"Awwww, what a cute dog!"

"Ooooh, adorable!"

"What's his name?"

All this fawning and questioning is happening at once.

I hold Peach up in front of me like a lion-cub in a Disney movie and tell them, "This is Princess Peach, she's a small-breed mutt."

She wags her tail, pleased with all the attention.

"She is so precious! How old is she?"

"I think she's around five years old. I adopted her from the shelter when she was already grown, so I'm not sure."

As I talk with all these naked women about my dog, I look at them and realize that we are all very different. Different accents, hair, and skin tone. Tall, short, fat, skinny, senior citizens, teenagers, and everything in between. There is nothing that we all have in common as to why we were abducted. Except that we're all women. What could this mean?

It can't be good.

"Girl." It's the voice of reason. I glance toward her to see that she is very pretty and very young with dark brown skin and short-cropped hair. Her eyes are big and very wide as she looks toward me. "Your alien is waking up."

"Oh, Jeezus!" Karen yells.

I feel a tentacle slide across my hip and wrap around my naked waist, then I'm yanked backward into the clawed grip of the alien.

CHAPTER SEVEN

—LU—

I have been captured by Seereechees again. This time I am caged with my human and her animal in the storage bay of a Seereechee ship. It is more crowded than when I was here last, with human females staggered about in individual cages, all naked. I would have never thought anything about the way other life forms clothe themselves before my time on Earth. My people, Homeworlders, do not wear any sort of coverings. Most everyone that I have traded with in person, whether furred, scaled, or smooth like a Seereechee, wear little to no clothes.

But humans do. Humans will cover their forms from their necks to their strange little toes and even wear tiny coverings on their heads at times.

It is strange to see all these human females with their skin bared, without any coverings or adornments. I know now that this is not their natural state, and they are unwillingly exposed. That is why I immediately worked to cover my human's form when I woke up. Wrapping many tentacles completely around her, trying to keep her covered. I only succeeded in startling her. I could taste her distress at being uncovered, but for some unknown reason, she grew even more distressed when I covered her up.

"Stop it, you!" She yelled at me, berating me in front of her fellow humans. Then she slapped one of my tentacles, right on one of the sensitive cups along the underside.

I have overstepped. I assumed she would prefer not to be exposed like this when all humans work diligently to keep themselves covered.

Perhaps she finds my touch distasteful? She would not be alone in this feeling. Most sentients in the known universe revile my kind, keeping their distance and avoiding all contact. It was too much to hope that this one would be different. Just because I admire her does not mean she feels this way toward me.

Holding my hands up in a universal 'not a threat' signal, I move all my tentacles back away from her, as far as I can in this small space. I look off to the side, as looking at her directly for any length of time could be interpreted as aggression.

"Awww, poor guy, you've hurt his feelings!" This is from one of the caged humans in front of us.

How could she know? I made an effort to keep my dermis from changing color with emotion. When I look down at myself though, there is a blue cast to my gray coloring.

"He just grabbed me. With his tentacles," my human argues.

"He looks so sad!" Another human observes.

"It's okay, octopus-guy. She's not mad." Another adds.

My human turns to face me, and gives me a considering look then says, "I'm not mad at you. You just startled me is all."

I nod to indicate my understanding.

"He understands you?" one of the humans asks, aghast as if I have trespassed on their conversation.

"Yes," my human answers, "but he can't speak."

"I most certainly can speak," I object.

"Oh, that must be his alien language," another one observes.

"He can understand English, but can't speak it," someone off to the side observes. "He may not be physically able to."

"I'm Gloria," my human introduces herself, pointing at her upper chest.

I very carefully enunciate the name given to me by my human crewmate months ago, and answer, *Kuh-thoo-loo*," then point toward my own chest with one tentacle. I suddenly realize that humans would not introduce themselves this way and point with a clawed hand.

"Did he say Cthulhu?" one of the humans whispers lowly to another.

"He did."

"Okay, Cthulhu," Gloria says, "Can I call you Lu?"

I nod again. It is a very useful human gesture, this chin-dip nod.

A Seereechee drone enters the room and I attempt to draw its attention.

"Drone, these human females require coverings and access to the translation matrix," I demand.

"No."

"Humans cover themselves, they need clothing to maintain their mental and physical well-being."

"No."

Seereechee drones are not sentient. Not in the way that the rest of us in this room are. They have a hive mind that they are connected to. It has been theorized that there must be some sort of organic hub, a Seereechee drone queen, that directs all the drones on a ship and cuts off individuals who are captured or compromised. They can be reasoned with, but they never explain anything so there's no arguing with them. If the answer is 'no' that's it. No further statements or questions will sway them.

I think a moment and then say, "This female," I gesture toward Gloria with one tentacle, "needs a translation device if she is to be caged with me. For her safety and mine."

I watch as the drone quietly turns away from me and exits the storage bay. They did not say no, so perhaps they're retrieving a translation device. Or maybe my human and I will be separated.

I look around at all the human females chatting with each other though they are naked, caged, and separated. I can scent their distress and apprehension, but there is a facade of easy banter. Why are they expending this energy to act relaxed in a stressful situation? It could be that chatter is soothing to human females. As my eyes drift over this crowd, my gaze is snagged by something distinctly not-human caged along the far wall. It is an Arana-Vora, a dangerous predator. Arana-Voras can only survive on a diet of sentient life forms. They are vile and disgusting creatures.

My first instinct is to pull my human close and protect her from this new danger, but I stop myself. We are safe in this cage, and she has already made her unfavorable feelings about my touch plain. I force my tentacles to curl in on themselves and away from her.

The Arana-Vora is not attacking anyone. There is a human female in the cage with it, and I can see that she is alive. Unconscious, but living. If the beast was going to make a meal out of anyone, it would be the one conveniently left in its vicinity.

Arana-Voras can go up to fifteen years without eating anyone, I remind myself. This one is not necessarily a danger to Gloria or any of the other Earth females. I need to focus on more immediate issues. Like escape. I did it before. I am sure I can escape Seereechee enslavement again. And take Gloria with me.

Gloria did not react in abject horror to the sight of me. She was not terrified when I touched her. Startled and angry at my presumption, I think, but not paralyzed with fear as I assumed she would be. Perhaps, if I can get us free of enslavement and safe on my home ship, she might wish to stay with me. Why should she want to return to her overcrowded planet? Where she might be attacked by brutish males or kidnapped by dishonorable Seereechees at any time? I could take care of her and keep her safe.

All this time the human females have been chatting with each other in their adorable Earth language that sounds like the squeaks, peeps, and chirps of tiny woodland creatures. But they are suddenly quiet. And staring at me.

I freeze. What has happened that they would look at me this way? Then I glance at Gloria and see that while I was lost in thought, two of my tentacles had wound around her. One coiled at her torso, the other snaking around her lower leg.

I release her again, moving as far away from her as I can. I need to get control of myself.

I hear a bubbling chirp that translates to amusement, then another. Even Gloria makes an amused sound and says, "Those tentacles kind of do their own thing, don't they?"

I nod, embarrassed.

I have not been paying attention to our surroundings. I am surprised when the Seereechee drone appears again next to our cage. It has a clip-on translation device that it pushes through the cage wall. Gloria is immediately at the wall, checking its solidity, looking for a weakness where the clip was pushed through, but she will not find any.

"Gloria," I say to get her attention, but I am unable to speak those human sounds and the approximation that comes out does not get her attention.

Scooping up the translation device, I snag her hand with one tentacle, turn it palm up and deposit the metal clip there.

"This is for me?" she asks, squinting at it.

I nod. Pantomiming, I demonstrate that she should clip it to her cute little shell-shaped ear.

She does so and I draw a breath to speak to her now that she will understand, but I'm interrupted by human screeches.

Following the noises, waving hands, and pointing digits of the females I see the Arana-Vora outside of his cage, cradling the unconscious human in one arm and stabbing a Seereechee drone in the ear with the dagger-sharp tip of a foreleg. It hisses and chitters at the dying drone, standing half out of its cage, the force field offering zero deterrence to its escape.

As I realize that we are all in terrible danger from this beast, it turns its gaze toward me. I swear its glowing red eyes spark with recognition and as it moves in my direction. I grab my human and force her behind me.

Then the fog descends.

CHAPTER EIGHT

—GLORIA—

It looks like we're in time out again. But this time is a lot worse because I can hear all the other women yelling and shrieking about that giant spider getting loose. And there is a tapping sound that might be clawed spider feet hurrying from the far side of this giant room closer to my side. I'm creeped out, but not terrified. Not screaming like all these other captives. I mean, sure, the spider is scary, but it's a prisoner like us. And it hadn't done anything to that unconscious woman in its cage. So, it's probably not going to bother any of us. And that gray alien it killed, well, they had it coming, didn't they? The kidnapping bastards.

Lu has wrapped his tentacles around me again, but this time I don't get on his case about it. It's helping me feel secure and grounded, not so vulnerable, and naked. I don't know what I've done to earn it, but this giant tentacled alien seems to feel protective of me. So, he's holding me and I'm holding Peach then I hear something strange.

Whistling. Like a bird mimicking a song, but even prettier and more melodious. And, in my head, I know what the whistles mean. It says, "Lu, I am glad to find you."

Lu hiccups loudly, but I understand that too.

"Baht?" And I know it's a name.

"Yes, we must escape," the whistling continues, but I can't focus on the music of it because I'm hearing it immediately translated. "Leave that human and her animal for now and I can get you out of there."

"No."

This is so weird. I'm listening to a conversation in two different alien languages.

"You are honorable to worry for these humans, but we will come back and free them. We must free ourselves first."

It's a sound argument. Weirdly.

"I said the same to Ken when I escaped. I haven't seen him or those he was imprisoned with since," Lu argues back.

Oh, poor guy. I guess he had already escaped from here once and now he's been recaptured.

There is a high whistle that I interpret as frustration.

"Fine. Bring your human with—come now."

I'm yanked through the cage wall, but it's not solid anymore. It's tingly gelatin that I'm pulled firmly into then out of.

When we're out of the cage, there is no fog. I can see all the other women, but I can tell that they can't see me. I guess that fog only works inside the cages? I can't see it, but it must still be there.

I hold Peach tightly as I'm carried out of the cavernous room and down a hallway. We encounter more of the gray aliens and the spider guy immediately murders them, stabbing them in their heads with a pointy forelimb. It's pretty jarring how violent these aliens can be, not hesitating to murder people left and right.

And another thing. Baht, the alien spider, is carrying the unconscious woman from his cage in one of his long spidery arms. He didn't leave her behind. But he told Lu to leave me? What a hypocrite!

As I'm thinking these uncharitable thoughts, we are leaving a trail of dead aliens in our wake. We keep encountering them, and Baht keeps killing them without slowing down.

Stab! A dead gray alien falls to the floor. Stab! Another dead alien. Stab!

Lu even gets in on the murderous action when a group of

four grays round a corner. He shifts me behind him, but I look around him to watch as he snatches up two grays in his tentacles and bangs them together with such force that their heads kind of—explode?

Alien blood and brains rain down over all of us.

It's a bit much.

"Twist their necks next time," our spidery accomplice whistles. "This mess is unnecessary."

"I am not practiced at violence." Lu sounds indignant.

He seems practiced at killing. He didn't hesitate at all. And he told me about murdering those guys back at the beach house in the same way.

"Practice now."

The spider grabs another gray but doesn't stab the side of his head. He braces the alien's shoulder with one limb and twists its head with another. There's a muffled snap and then the dead thing falls to the floor.

"Like so."

Lu takes this lesson to heart and starts dispatching our gray enemies with violent precision as we go, taking turns with Baht until we arrive...at a wall.

Lu touches it with a tentacle tip and an electrical shock zings through his body, mine, and Peach's. My poor little dog lets out a yelp.

"Apologies." Lu has regret in his voice and he pets my head gently. What a weirdo.

"Stand back," Baht whistles.

"Wait," Lu says, "Allow me to hold that human."

"Not necessary."

"I will keep her safe while you go through first."

Baht eyes us and with this pause, I get a good look at him.

He has long, hard skinny legs, exactly like a spider. But his torso and head are kind of human-ish. It's hard to tell because his coloring is a deep, flat black and his eyes are a glowing red. The glow obscures his features. But what I can make out of those features looks human. Sort of.

"Agreed." Baht hands the woman over to Lu, who cradles her gently in two tentacles.

She looks sick, with lank oily hair, dry cracked lips, and sunken eyes. And it's a bad sign that she hasn't woke up this whole time.

In my peripheral vision, I see Baht rush the wall, and then all the lights go out and the alien's glowing red eyes are the only thing I can see as he moves through the place where the wall used to be and into the room beyond.

It's really hard to see in there.

"Come." Baht orders us and Lu complies, moving through without a problem now.

There is a really big animal or something in this room. I can hear its gasping breaths and feel warm humidity radiating off its body.

"Baht," Lu says quietly.

"Silence."

"But the ship is shut down. It is falling from orbit and the environment—"

"Silence you, weak-bodied fool. Shut your stupid mouth."

Well. Rude.

As we quietly inch across this room, I can hear the gasping breaths of whatever is in here with us. I feel the wet air moving against my face.

Baht must have closed his glowing eyes because everything goes truly dark.

And then the screeching starts, so loud and grating that it hurts. Hurts a lot. I cover my ears only to feel a warm fluid start to leak out of them. My eardrums must have burst from that terrible noise.

Now it's quiet. Really, really quiet.

Oh, fuck have I lost my hearing? Like entirely?

I am freaking out. My ears and my whole head hurt and I'm crying.

The lights snap on and...I just can't even describe the sight. The far wall of the room, I don't even know how big it is, but it seems to be alive. Or was alive. It's all bumpy, made out of skin the same color as those gray bastards.

What is it even? My mind just refuses to make sense of what I'm looking at. Whatever the fuck it is, Baht is killing it. And, um, eating it? There is like, a fleshy vent that seems to be where this thing breathes. Baht is tearing at it, drinking and chewing, and obviously ingesting whatever the hell this thing is.

Oh, my God. I just can't. I look away.

Thankfully, Lu turns and leaves the room, carrying me and the other woman away from the horrific scene.

What just happened? Obviously attacking that thing turned the lights back on. Hopefully, that means we aren't going to crash.

We arrive in a room that has a table and a large tank. Everything in the room is white, but kind of shiny except for the tank which is blue. Or maybe the liquid in the tank is blue and the tank itself is clear. Lu looks at me and then the other woman and then back at me. He seems to be trying to make some kind of decision. His mouth moves, but I can't hear him at all. He breathes out a sigh. Then he sets me down to sit on the table and hauls the other woman up to the tank. He pulls something down from the ceiling and fastens it to her face then plops her into the tank. It's not liquid, I can see that now. It's more like blue gelatin. She is hanging suspended in it.

My brain isn't working at all right now. I'm seeing everything that's happening, but I can't interpret it. My body feels kind of floaty and disconnected. Lu starts wrapping his tentacles around me again, picks me up, and holds me against his chest. His body seems to vibrate in a soothing way that makes my muscles relax.

Before I know it, I'm closing my eyes and falling asleep.

CHAPTER NINE

—LU—

Baht finds us in the Medbay.

I have known Baht for spans. He was the very first person we established a trade relationship with when we left Homeworld 2. My crewmates and I had no experience with people outside of our own species. We could not know how strange Baht is. That it was not normal that he kept himself covered by a bulky cloak at all times. It was strange and suspicious that he spoke only Urglassi. Urglassi are tiny, winged people. Now we know, it is obvious to us that it's not his native language.

Looking at him, towering over me and hissing in rage, I do not understand how I could have been so completely tricked. How did he fold those long, bony legs up under his cloak? How could this being who is twice as tall as me squish himself up so small?

Seven suspected it. I do not know how he figured it out. I remember being incredulous when he suggested to me that our trade partner could be a bloodthirsty, bestial Arana-Vora. Even though I knew his arguments made sense, I could not take him seriously.

Arana-Voras are dangerous for two reasons. The first and most obvious is that their diet consists of sentient creatures consumed live. They do not have to eat often, they can go spans and spans without and survive. But they are always hungry. Even if they have just eaten, even as they are eating, they are starving.

An Arana-Vora will never be sated from any meal. Also, they are notoriously difficult to kill. They do not require implants because they have a natural affinity for the AI systems that run ships. They can overcome fail-safe, bypass security measures, and it has even been theorized that they can interfere with the neural implants all travelers have. How can you defend yourself against something with no weakness? How can I keep myself and Gloria safe from this starving, enraged monster?

"Where is she?" The beast hisses in my face in his native language. No longer the melodious whistles of Urglassi, this is the nerve-grinding Voranish chitter.

I try to hold myself with dignity. If this is how I am to die, consumed by this fiend, I will not scream or cower. I will not abase myself before one who deceived me and pretended to be an honorable friend when he is truly a Void-sent monster.

"She is in the regen tank." I gesture toward his human with one tentacle. "Her heart had stopped beating. She had not taken a breath in—"

He slides past me to the tank and braces two forelimbs against the clear plexi-shield, obviously ignoring me.

I had planned to wait a few hours until that human had recovered. Assisted by regen goop, it should not even take that long. Then I would put Gloria in the tank. Her ears are injured. I observed bloody fluid leaking from them. And her eyes were leaking some sort of water.

While Baht has his back to me, I worry over whether Gloria and I are safer with him, or should I break for another part of the ship? Maybe I can find another regen tank, some ships have two.

"Can you—" Baht starts in chittering Voranish. He pauses, seems to collect himself, and continues in whistling Urglassi, "Lu, would you please go and retrieve a cloak for me?"

I receive an image via my neural implant, it's a map instructing me to go to the industrial fabricator in a storage bay and retrieve a cloak that Baht has printed up. As reluctant as I am to displease Baht, and as much as I would like to see his monstrous form covered, I cannot.

I wave one tentacle toward Gloria. "She is unwell. I do not want to jostle her at all. And what if I encounter drones?"

"The drones will not interfere with us."

I just take in that mysterious statement. There must be thousands of Seereechee drones on this ship. I heard that it only takes two hours to grow a Seereechee, that they aren't hatched or birthed but grown in vats. And a ship like this, well there is every reason to assume it is fully staffed.

He sees my disbelief and explains, "I am controlling the drones now."

I do not believe it and he can tell, so he goes on to explain.

"You know that my kind can only consume sentient life forms? Have you ever wondered why that is?"

Shrugging all my tentacles except the one holding Gloria, I answer, "Is it not a simple preference?"

"No. An Arana-Vora is changed by what he consumes. When one of my kind goes about consuming dumb animals they lose their sentience and intelligence. They will quickly become ani-malistic themselves, and for the good of all life in the universe, that cannot be allowed to happen. Can you imagine something as dangerous as I, being ruled by only hunger and aggression?"

I recoil in horror.

"I see that you understand."

He caresses a forelimb down the plexi-shield, following the line of the Earth-Human's face.

"They put this poor, sick little female into the cage with me because they knew I was starving to death. I have not consumed a meal in thirty spans and was at the end of my life. That was fine. I am not a good person. My life is not worth more than anybody else's and I doubt a single person in this universe will mourn my loss."

What do I say to this? I have always liked Baht, and even though I have learned this terrible truth about him I still con-sider him a friend. But who would I sacrifice to save him? Every-body knows that Seereechee drones are not sentient and there-fore unfit for an Arana-Vora to consume.

"So they tried to feed her to me. Idiots! It ruined my whole plan. Lu, it was a masterful plan to get myself sold to Seereechees at a slave market and then infiltrate their ship's systems and figure out—"

He interrupts himself with a frustrated sigh and continues.

"But I could not just let her die, you understand that, right?"

I nod, though I do not understand.

"She was ill from the start, but they would not give her any food or water. They would not take her to a medbay. They said it would be a waste! The heartless bastards!"

I have to ask, "A Seereechee drone said this to you?"

"No," he looks at me like I am the incomprehensible one. "The Shentfer traders."

Ugh. Gross. Shentfers are awful, unhygienic pirates and scavengers.

"Those Seereechees folded us directly from the trade grounds."

To travel long distances, a fold in space must be created. A ship will enter the fold at the point of origin, then exit the fold in the same moment at their destination.

"How do you mean? Was your shuttle pre-programed—""

"You misunderstand," he interrupts. "We did not fold from our end. The Seereechees created an inverted fold that pulled us through. No shuttle, no protective gear. Just bodily pulled us through."

I gape at him. This is unheard of. How can anyone survive?

At that moment, a Seereechee drone enters the room.

I sweep Gloria's unconscious body behind me and grab the drone to snap its neck in a practiced, fluid motion.

As it falls to the floor, a piece of fabric comes unfolded from its lifeless arms.

It's a cloak.

Baht kicks the corpse away, snatches the cloak and dons it. His long legs fold and adjust tightly to his body and he is the trader I know again. Shorter than I, all covered and bundled with only his eyes showing.

"You do not need to worry about the drones on this ship," he states calmly. "They are under my control."

I do not know what to say to this. Perhaps he has gone mad.

"All Seereechee drones are controlled remotely," he explains.

"Yes," I agree. "By a Seereechee Queen. Baht, are you telling me you think you are a Seereechee Queen?"

He huffs a laugh and says, "Almost."

I cover my face with my clawed hands. This is too much. Baht is too dangerous to be crazy on top of it. How can I be expected to deal with this deteriorating situation?

"Lu, listen, you were there," he tells me. "You saw me consume their Queen."

I recoil from him and ask for clarification, "That thing? That wall in the room was…"

"Well, it was not the whole queen, just the most important part. I was surprised to learn that Seereechee queens are a quarter the size of their ships and reside at the very center."

"How— What? How did you learn this?"

"By accessing the ship maintenance schedules."

This is too much. I can only deal with so much and the idea that Baht, an Arana-Vora, is now a Seereechee Queen? It is too ridiculous! It makes no sense!

"By consuming their queen, I took on the hive-mind aspect of a Seereechees lived experience." He gestures toward the dead drone. "Here is an example. I wanted a cloak and this drone brought it. I did not order them to. I did not think 'I need a drone to bring me a cloak.' When I asked you to retrieve the cloak, the drone acted as an extension of my will and brought it."

"Apologies for killing your drone," I offer.

He just shrugs.

I take a fortifying breath "All of this explaining was to say that these drones are no longer a threat. They work for you."

"Exactly."

"And you are no longer dying of starvation because you consumed their queen?"

"Yes."

"So this ship and everything on it now belongs to you."

He tilts his head in agreement.

"What are you going to do with all of those females?"

His whole body gives a start, and his glowing red eyes widen. "I had forgotten about them."

"You should release them."

"Yes. Of course. I am not a slaver, Lu." He huffs again.

"You did not absorb that aspect?"

"No! I am still," he shakes his head, "I am myself. I take on the abilities, not the personality."

"I am glad."

I do not believe him. He already told me that Arana-Voras are changed by what they consume.

He walks over to the wall and a cabinet pops open so he can retrieve something from inside. It's an injecting device.

"What are you doing with that?" I ask.

"Assisting your human," he replies as he fills the injector with regen goop then hands it to me. "Put some on the outer and inner area affected. It should be enough to heal her injuries in a few moments."

Gloria's ears are like tiny little funnels. Applying the goop is easy.

"A shuttle is being assembled to ferry all of the humans back down to their planet."

"All of them?" I ask.

"Well, not this one." He gestures toward the regen tank. "I will return her if she asks, but she needs care so she can recover from her ordeal."

I wave toward Gloria. "That is true for this one as well."

He tilts his head, assuming a perplexed attitude. "She is already recovered."

I am sure he is correct, but... "She might be recovered physically, but she has been through a terrible ordeal. She needs to recover emotionally." I am making up this argument as I go. I just want to keep her with me.

"You will help her recover emotionally?" he asks. "You feel

qualified to do this? More qualified than her fellow humans?"

"Yes," I lie. He lets it go.

CHAPTER TEN

—GLORIA—

Someone put me in a bikini. That's the first thing I notice when I wake up. It's red with white polka dots. I can feel that it's not exactly the same as other bathing suits I've worn. It's smoother, has no bumpy seams, and has no liner. And the material is kind of thick, but it's light and kind of, well, squishy? It's comfortable though, breathable, and it fits well. But why am I wearing a bikini? I look around me to find I'm in a very strange room. No windows, no door. The walls and ceiling are a very light, dull metallic kind of material and the floor is made out of stuff like foam mats, but it's the whole floor and seamless. And the light is strange. There's no source, soft light seems to be coming from everywhere in the room. I mean, there's no lamps anywhere and I'm not casting any shadow. The light must just be coming from everywhere, right?

I push myself up to stand and that's when I realize I was sleeping on a pile of blankets. Weird. Everything about this situation is frickin weird! Including this swimsuit!

It seems like no matter how surreal my life gets lately, it always gets weirder.

There is noise to the left and I'm startled to see that there is in fact a door and it's just whisked open. One of those gray aliens comes into the room.

I scramble back into the corner, but they just pull a cart in behind them. I squeeze as far into the corner as I can. They don't seem to take any notice of me, as their sole focus is the cart.

The door remains open, and the gray alien isn't even looking at me. I make a split-second decision and dash out of the room. Full tilt, I'm running down space-ship corridors. My hair is streaming behind me, and this bikini obviously has zero support because I'm extra bouncy as I run. I take every single turn I come to, and I have no idea where I'm going, just a vague notion that I should get free, find a way out. There are gray aliens all over the place, moving with purpose and not even noticing me.

Now I'm feeling kind of silly.

Nobody is trying to catch me. I'm just running myself out of breath for no reason. Slowing to a walk to catch my breath, I glance all around.

I wonder where Lu is. Why did he make such a big deal out of keeping me with him and then just leave me? Turning, I check every direction, half-expecting to find him standing behind me. But he's not.

What are these aliens doing anyway? There is no order to it. They are just walking from one door to another. Some are carrying things, a tray of bowls filled with noodles, a blanket, and other things that I can't even identify.

Then I hear a bark. Peach! How could I have forgotten about her? I don't even know when I lost track of her!

I'm the worst dog mom.

I follow the sound and see one of the gray aliens carrying her off as Peach looks over their shoulder and yaps excitedly, wagging his tail.

"Hey!" I yell. The alien doesn't hear me. "Hey, you with my dog! Get back here!"

The alien turns and walks through a door that opens to his right. I'm jogging to catch up and slide through the door quickly, so it doesn't close on me. I arrive just in time to see the alien hand my dog off to—Karen?

"Hey!" I yell again. "Karen!"

She doesn't have that querulous look on her face when she catches sight of me. She looks...relieved.

42

"Oh, thank goodness!" she says as she runs over and hands me Peach. "We were so worried when you left with those aliens!"

She gives me a quick hug, squeezing me tightly as I stand there in shocked silence. This is another weird experience, being hugged by a naked woman. But it's kind of nice that she was so worried.

Grabbing my shoulders, she stands back to take a look at my bikini.

"Where did you get this?"

"I don't know!" I yell at her and her eyes widen in alarm. "Sorry, it's just this has been the single craziest day of my life! And the aliens just keep killing each other! And I woke up alone! I didn't know where I was or how to get back!"

I might be losing my shit a little bit.

"Shhhh," Karen soothes me, patting my back. "Honey, it'll be okay, don't worry." She starts leading me farther into the room and I can see now that all of the abducted women are here. They aren't in any kind of cages, just milling around. "Listen, they let us all out and brought us to this room. See?" She gestures around at everyone who's silently staring at us. "We are all okay. And one of those grays said they're getting a shuttle ready to take us back to Earth. Now, isn't that good news?"

I nod my head and let her coddle me as all the shock and fear I've experienced comes to the surface. She steers me toward a corner, patting and soothing me the whole time. I sit against the wall, and she sits next to me until I am calmer.

"So which aliens got murdered? The spider one? Your tentacle friend?" she asks.

"No." I gasp. "They—" I take a shuddering breath. "They killed grays! So many of them! Stabbing and bashing and twisting their heads around!" I'm getting worked up again. I take another breath trying to calm and center myself before I continue. "At least twenty of them. And then there was this monstrous thing! It was so huge, it was like a wall! And that spider-alien, Baht, he killed it and ate part of it! It was so disgusting, I just can't—"

"Shhhh. It's okay. You don't have to keep talking about it. Look, as far as we can tell there has been some kind of mutiny. Or maybe just a change in management. But whoever's in charge now is sending us home. Soon this will all be a crazy memory that we can't tell anyone. Who will believe it?"

I continue focusing on breathing and calming down, but I don't feel well. My body feels kind of floaty, but my head feels heavy. I've never been emotionally out of control like this.

A warm smooth hand grabs my wrist and I look to the side to see a young woman. It's the reasonable one. I never got her name. Right now, she is obviously taking my pulse. I don't know how she can do that without a clock. Don't you need to count and keep time?

She lets go but then grabs my shoulder, turning me toward her, and peers into my eyes, first one then the other. Her dark, expressive eyes are concerned, but calm. Cupping my shoulders, she moves her palms down my naked arms then squeezes my hands when she reaches them.

"I think you're in shock," she says.

I nod. That makes sense.

"Are you hurt at all? In any pain?"

I shake my head then say, "My ears were damaged, but they seem fine now. And I was shocked. With electricity."

"Any burns?"

"No."

"Ok, well I need you to lie down on the floor and elevate your legs." she moves me around and I allow her to reposition me. "Let's rest your legs here. You don't mind, do you?" she asks Karen as she drapes my legs over Karen's lap.

"Not a bit."

"Ok. then," she wipes her hands on her thighs. "I'll go see if I can find a blanket for her."

It is only minutes later when another Gray enters the room.

"Earth-Humans," he addresses us loudly from the door. "Follow. A shuttle is ready to return you to your planet's surface."

I get up too quickly and it makes me dizzy, but Karen lends

me a hand and leads me out of the room with her.

There's a bottleneck of naked women waiting around the side of the shuttle, and it gives me a moment to take a look at it and start to feel apprehensive. It looks very new. Did they just make this shuttle today? How do they know it will work safely? Do they even care if it does? We could all burn up in the atmosphere if this thing—

"Hey, shhhh." Karen is rubbing my back again. "It's all right. They make these shuttles all the time and it's perfectly safe. One of the Grays explained it before you came back."

I nod my head and feel silly. I need to get ahold of myself.

A Gray hands me and Karen blankets that are thin, but soft and warm and we quickly wrap ourselves in them and move toward the shuttle. It just looks like a rectangular box with rounded corners and a large hole in one side. I can see through the hole that there are rows of seats.

The uneasy feeling returns. It's a mistake to board this thing, I know it. But what else is there to do? Just stay here and live with creepy aliens for the rest of my life?

There are straps on the seats, but no buckles, and when I sit down the straps on either side just come together like magnets, and now it looks like it's all one piece and always has been. I wonder how I'll get out of this seat when we land? Karen hands me Peach. When did I let her go? I can't remember. I tuck the little dog under the straps and under my blanket so only her face is sticking out.

The door closes slowly from both sides, the wall just seems to magically expand to cover the opening, and right before it closes completely Lu, my giant tentacled alien comes through the doorway. His eyes zero in on me. I only have a glance at him before I can't see anymore because we are totally enclosed in this shuttle.

He looks stricken.

Is he upset that I'm leaving? Didn't he know about the shuttle?

I'm going to miss him. He's a nice guy, for a monstrous alien.

There is a *click* sound, then a kind of *shhhleppp*, and then we are falling. I feel that lifting, floating feeling, like when an elevator starts moving down, only a hundred times worse.

The women all seem to start talking at once and my anxious brain is screaming at me. We are falling through the sky! From space! This isn't safe! We could all die!

Karen is gripping my hand, deathly tight.

Then that falling feeling tapers off and we aren't moving anymore. I can feel that we are still and on the ground. And alive.

All of the walls fall away and float to the ground and our restraints fall off our bodies and off the seats. The seats themselves start to crumble and then we are all just standing among debris that is crumbling to dust and blowing away.

We are in a plowed field. It's all furrowed dirt, no plants yet.

Add this to the list of unbelievable things that have happened today. Our shuttle just disintegrated.

And there are men all around us in a circle. They are in uniforms and helmets and they're pointing guns at us.

CHAPTER ELEVEN

—LU—

Tiny will not stop pestering me. She's bursting with questions about my stay on Earth that I barely understand and do not have answers to. She barely finishes asking one before she is on to the next:

"What was the weather like?"

"Did you watch any *tee-vee*?"

"Who won the election?"

"Did anyone see you?"

And on and on. At length. I finally accessed the visual files from my implant and projected the video feed onto the wall of a security alcove for her to peruse at her leisure, but even then, she was full of demands.

"Pause here."

"Fast forward, please."

"Wait, rewind a sec."

"Who's the girl?" she asks, lightly nudging her shoulder into my arm. "This kayaking girl you keep watching?"

"Gloria," I answer simply. It is unlikely these two women know each other, what with Earth being so populous.

"Glo-ree-ah," Tiny stretches the name out as though savoring it. "I like it." She peers closely at the video again. "She's cute too. And look at that adorable little dog!"

"Princess Peach."

"Adorable!" She sighs and clasps her hands together in front of her chest. There is a shimmery red cloth wrapped around her shoulders, chest, and hips. It crisscrosses around her body so that she is modestly covered, as humans like to be.

She is engrossed. Looping her arm through mine, she demands, "Fast forward through all of the hunting, eating, and sleeping please."

I do so with a shrug. I rather thought that the hunting parts were interesting.

She gasps and grips my arm tightly. We have arrived at the part where those criminal males attacked Gloria and tried to steal her away.

"Oh no!" she protests as one of the criminals kicks Princess Peach across the yard.

And then she watches me kill those two human men. Baht was correct in his assessment. It is an unnecessarily messy and dramatic way to murder people. There is blood and brain matter splashed all around.

I glance down at Tiny, and she is staring at me in slack-jawed surprise.

"You killed those guys."

"Yes."

Her arm remains looped in mine, but where she was holding me next to her a moment ago now her hand is resting limply on my forearm. What does this mean? Is she disgusted by my actions? I have not come to terms with it myself.

She gasps again. "She thinks you hurt the dog!"

I remain with her for the next hours as she reviews all the footage. Seven, who is apparently Tiny's breed-mate now, comes to check on her three times. Each time she humors him for a few minutes then shoos him away.

"You know...she looks familiar. I think I know her from somewhere."

"That is unlikely."

Nodding, she watches the last hours, fast-forwarding through most of it.

"Why did you make a bikini for her?" she asks, puzzled.

"Humans prefer to be covered," I remind her. "This is her preferred covering."

"Really?"

"Yes."

"Lu, she wore bikinis by the pool and kayaking at a beach house. She was on vacation. I doubt she wanted a bikini to hang out on a Seereechee spaceship."

"Oh." That makes sense. My mood plummets even more, to think that Gloria must have been unhappy about the *bikini* when she woke up. I thought that was something I had done right for her.

She tugs me away from the security alcove and toward the cafeteria.

"Let's go have some lunch and talk about Gloria."

I do not know if there is anything to talk about, but it is nice being with Tiny. She's very chatty, and all the talking fills a void. I have not been myself since my return. Everything feels pointless. I was relieved to be back at first, happy that my whole crew seems to be fine. We are recovered from our arrest and enslavement. I was able to synch my neural implant with the ship's security feed and learned that my podmates and I had been detained and arrested by bounty hunters. We had been knocked out and then kept in cryo-detention, unaware of any of it. But after Tiny secured our release, Ken and I were intercepted by Seereechee slavers while still in cryo-stasis. That explains that. It also explains why Baht was there. He was in on the plot to free us.

So now Ken, Seven, and I do not need to worry about the laws of Homeworld Two anymore. We have been officially banished, stripped of our rights and property, totally free though.

I was surprised to learn that our ship had been awarded to Tiny in a misguided attempt by the government of Homeworld Two to placate her. Ridiculous. She does not even have the neural implants to pilot a shuttle much less this whole homeship.

"So," she draws my attention as we bring our noodles to a table. "This girl is special?"

"Yes."

"And you wanted to keep her? That's what you told Baht."

I dip my chin in affirmation.

"Then why didn't you invite her to come here with you?" She chews a bite of noodles waiting for my answer. She had Ken fabricate a stick with claws on the end to compensate for her woeful lack of talons. Humans have flimsy, delicate claws that are not good for much other than decoration.

"Lu?"

"I did not have a chance. I left her unconscious in a private room while I searched for her animal companion. She would have been distressed to find her gone. I caught her scent near the shuttle bay and when I tracked it, I found Gloria and the animal had somehow both found their way to the shuttle and were headed directly back to the surface," I explain. I thought this was clear in the video record.

"You could have stopped that shuttle. She had a translation device so you could have just asked her." Tiny is waving one clawless hand around, getting herself worked up over this. I know why I wanted Gloria to stay with me, but I do not know why Tiny feels so strongly about it. Perhaps she is lonely for other humans? That could be why she's disappointed that I didn't bring this one back to the Homeship.

When I do not respond, she chews her noodles for a moment and then asks, "Why were those guys trying to kidnap her?"

"I do not know."

She sets her fork down.

"Lu, we don't know if she's safe, then."

This is a distressing thought.

She goes on, "And even if she's safe from kidnappers, what about the government? Do they know those women were abducted by aliens?"

"Earth does not have a government."

"We have lots of governments! And most of those governments have secret agencies that specialize in detaining people and getting information out of them."

Another distressing thought.

I shrug all of my tentacles to shake off these disturbing ideas that Tiny seems to be engendering in me on purpose. I had been working to be at peace with Gloria's decision to return to Earth. To respect her choice and not behave as some pirate, stealing her away and forcing her to stay with me against her will. But if she is being mistreated and it is for her own good that I track her down and abduct her away from Earth? That would be honorable would it not? She would be thankful for it.

"Tiny, Gloria knows as much about your Earth governments as you do. If she wanted to return to Earth, then…"

"But you didn't give her any other option!"

Breathing a deep, calming breath, I focus on changing my color from a distressed blackest-gray to a lighter hue.

With infinite patience, I ask, "What would you have me do?"

"We should go get her."

I shake my head in negation. "No, we are not Seereechee slavers to just go and abduct whatever human we like."

"You're right it wouldn't be right to just steal her away."

Glad to be in agreement, I dip my chin.

But then she adds, "We'll track her down and invite her aboard."

CHAPTER TWELVE

—LU—

"Ok, so step one: find Gloria." Tiny has a pencil and is writing in shimmery blue on the cafeteria table. The writing is an Earth-Human script that I cannot read. She finishes writing a line of indecipherable symbols and then looks around the table at each of us in turn.

"We should consider," Ken says, "whether we must find this specific human."

"What do you mean?" Tiny asks.

"Well, there are billions of humans. You explained that to me. That your whole planet swarms with humans. And almost half of them are female."

Tiny nods.

"It will be near impossible to find one human among billions. Could we not just land a shuttle and take the first human female that wanders near?"

Tiny sets her pencil down and looks at Ken for a moment before responding.

"Gloria is special. And she needs our help. She's the specific person we want to go get. We aren't just filling a human quota."

Ken dips his chin in agreement, but says, "Perhaps though, we should consider that every sentient being is a special individual and from what I have observed most of them need help. If Lu wants a human, we can just—""

"Jeez, Ken, do you really not get it?"

"Get what?" Seven, Ken, and I glance at each other. None of us *get it*.

"We are friends right, Ken?"

"Yes, of course."

"Ok, so if I was missing, if I was in trouble, and needed you to find me, would you? Or would you just go pick up some other human to replace me?"

Seven has snaked a tentacle around Tiny's waist and bares his fangs at Ken over her head. Any slight or threat to Tiny, even something that only upsets her mood engenders extreme reactions in Seven. I flash back on how violently I responded when Gloria was threatened, but I dismiss this line of thought. Seven is Tiny's breedmate. Gloria and I do not have that kind of relationship, so my feelings were out of line.

My tentacles all scrunch up and still, waiting for Ken's answer.

He says, "Of course we would find you."

"Ok, well, it's the same kind of situation with Gloria."

Ken holds up a tentacle to object. "But you do not know her. She is not your friend."

"She's Lu's friend!" Tiny is raising her voice in exasperation and Seven is snarling at Ken.

Ken looks at me, expecting me to comment on this.

"She is my friend," I answer, not exactly sure if I am being honest. Does Gloria consider me a friend? Or is this all wishful thinking on my part? In any case, if she is in trouble and being detained and mistreated as Tiny suspects, I will go find her whether Ken understands the why of it or not.

Tiny points her pencil toward the script she drew, "So, Step One: find Gloria."

"How will we find her, though?" Seven asks. "One human among billions?"

He holds both of his hands up peacefully because Tiny has whipped round to glare at him so fast that it caused her fluffy mane to bounce around her head. "I agree that we should find her," he explains placatingly. "I am wondering how."

"In the video Lu showed me, he gave her a translator. It's probably the only translator clip on Earth right now. Can we track that?"

I dip my chin to affirm. Even if it is not the only one on the planet, I should be able to track it because my neural implant had interphased with it while Gloria wore it.

Tiny scribbles some more of her Earth script then says, "Okay, so that's what we'll try first. If she's been detained, they probably took the clip. If the clip has been disabled or destroyed somehow, can we still track it?"

"No," Seven answers. "We need a signal. If there is no signal, we cannot track it."

We all sit quietly for a moment as Tiny scribbles some more. She is so energetic and creative. She is always making something.

Ken breaks the silence and says, "If the translation clip had interphased with a compatible device we could work out its location at the time it was disabled."

A good point, but Earth is so primitive I doubt any of their technology is compatible with a translation clip.

"Translation clips are very sturdy. I doubt a human could destroy it," Seven adds.

"Alright, so we'll operate on the assumption that we can track the translation clip. But when we find it, it probably won't be with Gloria," Tiny says, scribbling away. "So we need a plan for how we will get whoever we find with the translator to tell us where she is."

This is getting more complicated with every step.

"Even if they don't know where to find her, they should know something that will help us find her. Hopefully." She continues.

This is all starting to sound impossible. There are too many variables, and we are probably just going to get ourselves caught by these Earth government people. If they would detain people and treat them harshly just for having interacted with aliens, what might they do with any actual aliens they catch? It did not bear thinking about. But an idea comes to me.

"We need Baht's help," I say.

Seven says, "No." And glares at me.

"Where is Baht anyway?" Tiny asks, "I thought he would come back here when he was done infiltrating the Seereechee hive."

"He never said anything like that to me," I tell her. "Did he say that to you?"

"No, I guess not. I just assumed he was staying with us from now on. He seemed to like it here."

Tiny has a very sad cast to her face now. Did she really want Baht to stay with us on this ship forever?

She shrugs off her despondency and says, *"Double-yew, Double-yew, Bee, Dee,"* she writes emphatically as she talks. "What would Baht do?"

I understand half of her statement, but humans have many strange customs and ways of talking. It's best not to ask questions. Or answer questions since more than half of human questions are not real questions, but hypothetical ones.

"Well, if he was here, the first thing he would do is start sending polite messages asking for her back, and if that doesn't work, he would hire bounty hunters to retrieve her. If that didn't work, he'd go himself," Tiny explains, writing all of it down. She has nearly run out of room on this table.

"I did not say we need him to plan the rescue," I say. "We need him for his affinity with AIs and computer systems."

"But you have a point, Tiny," Ken says. "If we can track down that translator, one of us could interphase with it and use it to broadcast a message. We could just politely inquire about Gloria's whereabouts."

Seven adds, "And if they are disagreeable, we could inform them of the Seereechee threat that Earth is vulnerable to. We can tell them of Tiny's plan to protect Earth from this threat with an automated defense system."

Tiny nods. "That might soften them up." She continues writing. She has run out of room and is drawing a cramped script around the edges of the table.

"We will approach Earth again and track the translator clip. That is our first task in any case," Ken says.

"Agreed," Seven says. He then pulls Tiny close to him. He always has at least one tentacle loosely wrapped around her now and she does not mind. Seven's attention and his guarding behavior seem to make her glow with happiness. I never could have imagined such a thing, any being willingly submitting themselves to a Homeworlder's attention.

She smiles up at Seven, clasping his hand and interlacing her fingers with his. "Let's go check on the babies."

That is another thing. Tiny inexplicably allowed Seven to breed her, to seed spawn in her that she then diligently worked to guard and deliver safely. At great risk to herself. I would not have believed it, but I have reviewed the footage myself. I do not usually spy on others' breeding habits—none of us had any breeding habits to spy on until Tiny joined us.

I checked the security log because I was concerned that Seven may have manipulated or coerced her in some way. Historically, that is what Homeworlder spawning is, coercing an unwary being into hosting our young. That kind of behavior has been outlawed for centuries and nobody on Homeworld Two breeds in the old way anymore. There are fully automated artificial hosting chambers in breeding facilities on Homeworld Two. From the time an egg is harvested, through germination, until a youngling is ready to leave its tank and take on the responsibility and self-sufficiency of an adult citizen. The whole process is automated.

So, I was concerned. I could not believe that consent was given freely.

It was though.

I was shocked to see that Tiny had instigated their encounter. She had encouraged Seven at every juncture. Not just encouraged but demanded.

I am envious. Not that I have ever felt drawn to Tiny the way Seven is. But Seven has a breedmate. He has a willing host for his young. He is changed by it. Where he used to seem aimless, immature, and always in need of direction, now he is devoted and fierce in his focus on Tiny and the family he has made with her. He weighs options carefully then acts decisively.

I want that for myself.

Gloria's face surfaces in my mind, but I quickly discard that line of thinking. The very most I am to her is a friend. Just because Tiny feels romantic affection for one Homeworlder, does not mean that Gloria will follow suit. I suspect that Tiny is uniquely open-minded for a human. She would probably be considered a deviant among her kind for the choices she has made.

Everyone else has left the cafeteria and I am alone here with my thoughts, staring at the table Tiny has marked up. I need to shake myself out of this lassitude.

Ever since I first spied Gloria in her kayak, I have been struggling with my own wants. To be close to her. To guard her. I have wanted to touch her, breath in her scent, and keep her in my sight at all times.

I am proud of my restraint. But how can I maintain that restraint if Tiny succeeds in her plans and Gloria comes to stay with us on this ship?

CHAPTER THIRTEEN

—GLORIA—

"Ok, Miss Navarro, tell me again about the 'Spider Alien'."

Agent Howard is my least favorite agent. I don't know what agency she's with, but that's how she introduced herself, Agent Howard. She is always dressed casually, today it's jeans and a baby blue T-shirt. She has long, shiny blonde hair pulled back in a low ponytail and her big blue eyes are wide and blameless. "I'm just one of you girls," her look tells me, "You can trust me."

I frickin hate her.

It's been at least two weeks since I was rounded up with all the other abductees and we've all been detained in this facility. At least, I think we have. I haven't seen any of the other women in all that time.

And they took Peach.

I hate this fucking place.

"I've already told you. I've already told Chadwick and Smith and Johnson. I've repeated the same story at least fifty times," I say.

She has one of those babyish, little girl voices that some women have. And her way of speaking is overly cheerful. She explains, "The problem is that your story doesn't match up with the other abductees."

I shrug. I've answered them honestly. I'm not hiding anything.

"So the spider-alien—"

"I'm not answering anymore questions," I interrupt her. "I want a lawyer. I want to know why I'm being detained."

"You're not being detained, silly," she answers brightly. "This is quarantine."

I roll my eyes straight up to the ceiling and sigh.

"Seriously?"

"Yes," she's all eager earnestness, "you interacted with aliens. Who knows what sort of viruses, bacteria, or other microorganisms you might have picked up?"

"If I'm not being detained then bring me a phone so I can call my parents and my lawyer. I have the right to an attorney."

But, shit, even if she were to miraculously agree to bring me a phone, I don't have the numbers to call anybody. They are programmed into my cell. I haven't memorized any of them.

"No," Agent Howard argues in her silly, fake, annoying way, "Miranda Rights don't apply because you aren't under arrest. You have been admitted to this medical facility, not a prison."

"I better not get billed for this shit!" This concern pops out of my mouth as soon as I think it.

She laughs. This awful, annoying woman laughs at me.

"No, ma'am, you get free government healthcare here," she quips.

"Can I have that in writing?" I'm serious. Wouldn't it be just my luck if I get out of this situation somehow and I'm sent a $75,000 bill that wipes me out?

"I'll write it down for you when you leave," she promises, and it sends a shiver through my body. I can just tell that she doesn't expect I'll ever leave.

After Agent Howard gives up on interviewing me, she leaves through a security door. That door never opens for me, but it just opens right up when she walks to it. I know for sure there's some sort of video surveillance in here. I haven't seen an obvious camera anywhere and I wonder why they bother hiding them?

And what's with these agents? They all introduce themselves the same way: "I'm Agent blankety blank and I'll be interviewing you today." They've never said what agency they're with. And the only other person I've seen here is a silent male nurse. He's slim, around my height, 5'5", dishwater blonde hair, and gray eyes. He never speaks, not one word, as he takes my vitals and samples every day. One of the agents is always there for these checkups to boss me around, so the nurse doesn't have to say anything.

I've been trying to puzzle out why the nurse doesn't talk and all I came up with is that there must be a very specific script that the agents are following when they interview me, and the nurse isn't a part of it. Or maybe he has social anxiety. Or he could be mute.

I have a lot of time to think about the nurse and the agents because there is nothing to do here. No TV, no radio, no windows, nothing. I have a check-up in the morning, an interview after lunch, and then nothing. For hours, I'm here staring at the ceiling, pacing back and forth. Sometimes I do some exercises like lunges, jumping jacks, stretches, etc. But not often. I don't particularly enjoy it, so why add that unpleasantness to the tortures of solitary confinement?

I wonder how the other women are doing? Are they going through the same thing? I think maybe I'm getting particular treatment because I was up close with more aliens than the others.

I hope they were let go and made it home and are living their lives right now. I hold onto that happy thought extra hard even though I know it's unlikely.

My thoughts drift to Lu. I wonder what his home is like? Hopefully, he's all right wherever he is. I think about him a lot. It's not every day I make friends with an alien, after all. I should have stayed on that spaceship, not gotten on the shuttle. Everything happened so fast, and I was overwhelmed, but if I had thought about it, really weighed the pros and cons, I would have tried to stay.

I could be out in space right now. Lu seemed pretty attached to me. I don't know why, but he was very sweet and protective of me. For an alien. When I remember all of the things that went down and how violent it all was, one thing was constant: Lu kept me safe.

I lay on my bed and daydream. There's nothing else to do.

I've figured out a few things about my detention. The first thing is that these agents don't have any idea what to do with me. At first, I thought they were giving me the "white room treatment." You know, where the subject is deprived of stimulation to drive them crazy? My room here is all white. There are no windows or any form of entertainment or anyone to talk to. I don't have any shoes, just thick white socks with grippy tread on the bottoms. But the agents and the nurse have regular shoes that they wear these soft booties over. Everybody's steps are silent. In my mind, this all added up to sensory deprivation and it had me worried. Like, what other "enhanced interrogation techniques" are they going to try on me? And I'm not going to lie, it's getting to me. I'm bored out of my skull. But I don't feel tortured. And a couple of days ago I realized that it's not white room treatment because they're giving me regular food. Regular, colorful food. Peas, carrots, gelatin. Not rice, potatoes, or other bland fare. I listened with rapt attention to a podcast about enhanced interrogation (i.e., torture) a couple years ago and I remember specifically that the bland white food is a key factor.

So, they're giving me a half-assed, maybe accidental, white room treatment.

And the interviews are half-assed too. They don't care how I answer. They just talk to me for forty minutes then leave. Every day.

Those other enhanced techniques haven't happened either.

So, I'm just guessing, but it seems like there is no real plan where I'm concerned. No goals, no information they're trying to get out of me. Just routine. Just endless, boring detention.

I've had a lot of time to think. I think about the decisions I've made in my life that have lead me to this. I can be really hard on myself and if I'm feeling particularly down, I think that this could all have been avoided if I had been a better person. I could have stuck it out in college, went to med school, and made my parents proud. I didn't need to play video games and post on social media all the time. I didn't have to be so self-absorbed and attention-seeking. If I was living the kind of life I ought to, I wouldn't have been at that beach house by myself.

If I hadn't been so engrossed in recording video games walk throughs I would have never caught the attention of those Men's Rights guys. I had no idea the reaction I'd get at the time. I just made a joke about an NPC (non-player character) wearing skimpy clothes. She was wearing a tube top and shorts cut smaller than underwear. I thought it was funny to take few moments out of my walk-through and ask her if she needed help finding clothes.

I was just entertaining myself, it wasn't even really funny. But apparently it came across as scathingly witty feminist commentary on misogyny in video games. That's not how I meant it! But I couldn't really say that video games aren't misogynistic because they can be. You never see NPC men running around mostly naked.

A clip of that video ended up on TikTok where it was shared, duetted, and commented on more than a million times.

And then the worst part happened. The makers of the video game changed the NPC woman I had made fun of. They put her in jeans and a t-shirt. I never asked them to do that! Misogynistic or not, I like that game. But these Male's Rights Activists hated it and blamed me. And that's where all of the harassment, threats and everything started to spiral out of control.

These guys who are after me are no joke. It is ridiculous that they are so worked up over video game commentary. I didn't take it seriously at first. But I looked into them, and two shooting sprees have been attributed to groups affiliated with them. They are dangerous and I'm scared of them. Funnily enough, I'm safer here than I have been anywhere else since this started.

It's not worth it though. This detention is miserable and there's no end in sight.

Most of the time I try to be kind to myself. Aliens didn't abduct me because of my TikTok presence. They didn't know anything about my background before taking me. None of this is my fault.

To keep myself from spiraling into self-pity and self-doubt, I tell myself stories. Not out loud, I just imagine all kinds of scenarios in my head. I've made up backstories for all of the agents and the nurse. I've come up with all kinds of things that could be happening while I'm trapped in here. There could have been a coup. There could be guillotines erected in the streets. There could be a new, worse virus. Maybe I'm better off in here than out there, you know? Maybe a super volcano erupted. There could be wooly mammoths. I read an article a few months ago about how recent breakthroughs in gene editing now make it possible to resurrect extinct animals. No joke, look it up. There could be a wooly mammoth ranch down the road.

I'm not sure if all these wild imaginings are a healthy coping mechanism for a crazy situation or not, but I keep going with it. There is absolutely nothing else to do.

I go through every nutty scenario in my head, fleshing them out. Wild escaped mammoths rampage through downtown Atlanta. A super volcano erupts sending tons of ash into the atmosphere.

Anything could be happening. How would I know?

And my favorite story to tell myself over and over is the Alien Invasion. Not the gray aliens, the tentacle aliens. They arrive in force and invade Earth and I'm appointed as Earth's alien liaison because I have experience dealing with aliens. They give me back my translator and my dog. Peach and I go convince the aliens to give up their invasion and leave Earth in peace. And they invite me to leave with them and spend the rest of my life in space, visiting strange planets and having adventures. And of course, it's Lu who scoops me up in his tentacles and carries me onto his ship and into my new awesome life.

I've found that I can make stuff up and daydream for hours if I have to. It doesn't have to make sense.

When the interviews happen, they are getting kind of disjointed. I'm not even trying to hold it together anymore. Like, if they're trying to make me crazy then fine, I'll be crazy. I'll just lean into the crazy.

"Tell me about the gray aliens again?" They ask this question a lot. Gray alien, spider alien, tentacle alien. They just want me to keep talking about them.

"Gray aliens?" I ask, "I don't know. Maybe I imagined them. Aliens aren't real, are they?"

"No, you didn't imagine them. What do you recall about the gray aliens?"

I shake my head. "I've been imagining a lot of things lately. I probably made up those aliens." I tap the side of my head. "In my mind, you know? Maybe I'm imagining you telling me that I'm not imagining things."

"Ms. Navarro, three weeks ago you were abducted by aliens. There are many witness statements all attesting to this fact. You did not imagine—"

"Three weeks?" I raise my voice at him.

Agent Chadwick tilts his head in confusion or concern. I can't tell. "Yes, three weeks."

"That's not right." I'm shaking my head. "It must be a lot longer than that."

He's nonplussed for a moment. He pulls a phone out of his pants pocket and scrolls around for a second then says, "Yep, twenty-two interviews. That's three weeks and a day."

"What's the date?"

He just closes his phone and puts it away. No one will tell me things like the date, the time, the weather anything like that.

Chadwick is my favorite agent though because he lets his mask slip sometimes. Like how he took his phone out just now. And when I brought up white room treatment a few interviews ago, he laughed, a real spontaneous laugh, and said, "No. Darlin' you don't know anything about white rooms."

I just watched him for a second and he glanced around then said, "I see what you mean. Why you could think this is white room, but it's not. Not at all."

Then he got back to asking me about aliens.

I don't think the other agents have let themselves slip once. They don't genuinely laugh or smile.

He's continuing with his questions, asking about the same things they've asked over and over. I let my mind drift.

There is a loud slapping sound that is so jarring it takes me a moment to place it.

Plap! Plap! Plap!

And then I see that it's someone walking. Just walking in regular shoes on the tiled floor without booties. What the hell. It's so loud! This place is really, seriously messing with me.

I cringe with every step.

It's an older white guy with a gray mustache and a shaved bald head. He makes a waving gesture at Chadwick, and the agent leaves without a word. Then this new guy sits down. He's got a five o'clock shadow and wrinkles in his suit. Nothing like the agents I've been dealing with who are all cool as cucumbers and well-put-together. This guy is obviously harried and stressed.

"Ms.," he looks at a sheet of paper, "Navarro."

I nod.

"I'm here to brief you on some recent developments."

"Mammoths?" I ask excitedly.

He straightens and squints at me. Then says, "Young lady, I know you've been through some—"

"Enhanced interrogation?"

"Christ." He rubs a hand over his face. "No. You've been through some—" his eyes dart around the room as if the word he's looking for will be painted on the wall somewhere, "—disorientating experiences."

A single humorless laugh escapes me. "Huh. Yeah. Disorientating."

"Well, you need to snap out of it."

"Okay."

He gives me an assessing look, draws in a breath, then explains, "We've received a message—"

"Who's we?" I ask.

"The department."

"Which department?"

He sighs and that sigh is weighted with frustration. He closes his eyes and pinches the bridge of his nose.

"We have received a message," he starts over, "from an extra-terrestrial source."

"Neat."

Another silent, pinched stare, then he continues, "this extra-terrestrial source is demanding to speak with you."

"Wow."

"Indeed. we need you to get dressed and accompany us to—"

"No."

"Miss Navarro, you don't have a choice."

"Then why are you explaining things to me like you need my understanding and cooperation?" I ask, genuinely curious.

"This source seems to be under the impression that you would be willing to speak with them. That you have some kind of connection?"

Lu! It must be Lu and he came back for me! I try to keep a straight face and a cold expression.

"Meh."

"What? What does that mean?"

I fake a bored sigh then explain, "The last time I spoke with an extraterrestrial source I ended up in here. Detained. It's kind of been a raw deal for me. So I'm going to have to decline."

"Jeezus-fu—" he does another calming breath, "Ok, what do you want? How can I get you to this rendezvous?"

"I want my dog."

"Done."

"And I want some real clothes."

"Agreed."

"And my translator."

"Of course."

"And I want to be free. Free to go back to my old life when we're done."

He nods.

"Is that a yes?"

"Yes, when this is over you're free to go."

"Alright." I stand and stretch my arms overhead then shake them out. "Let's go rendezvous with aliens."

I change into an outfit Chadwick brings in and sets on the table. Khaki pants and a navy polo shirt and gray sneakers. Not my usual style, but it sure beats white scrubs and grippy socks.

Then I follow the bald guy out to the car. That's what I'm calling him. He never introduced himself and Chadwick calls him Sir, and I'm not going to call him that.

When we get outside, it's overcast, and I can't tell what time of day it might be. Day time. And we're in an office park. I didn't get a good look when we were brought in. But it's just a nondescript office park.

Bald Guy walks me to a gray sedan and Agent Howard is standing there holding Peach, who is happy as a clam, wagging her tail and yapping at me. Wherever she's been kept, she looks to have been well-cared for. She's groomed and a little fatter, so someone has been indulging her.

Howard hands her off to me and pats her head one time, saying, "She's a sweet dog."

I nod. I just really don't like Howard.

Bald guy taps the top of the car and says, "Let's go." Then gets in the front passenger seat. There's already someone in the driver's seat. I slide in the back.

And we're off.

CHAPTER FOURTEEN

—GLORIA—

So, this whole time I was expecting Lu to be the alien who was meeting us. Who else would contact the Department? What other alien even knows I exist? But it's not Lu who steps out of the shuttle to greet us.

The shuttle is very much like the one that brought me and all the other abducted women back to Earth. A big rectangular box with rounded corners and a doorway that just appears on the side. This one isn't disintegrating like ours did though and it's made out of a lighter, shiny material. And it's floating. Just floating about six feet off the ground. The ground is another freshly turned field. The car ride was around an hour and a half. I know because there's a clock on the dash of the car. I'm never going to take clocks for granted again.

This was a boring-ass car ride with the bald guy shuffling papers and going over information on the aliens as we rode.

"They call themselves Homeworlders. They are aligned with an Intergalactic Order of Federated Planets."

He's not talking to me, but Howard and the driver. I try to tune out and watch the scenery.

"The one we're meeting is a dedicated liaison. We couldn't get a name."

There's something soothing about all of these fields. It's lulling and hypnotic to drive past them.

"They are not aligned with the Grays. And the Grays are not

aligned with the Intergalactic Order of Federated Planets. These ones are new and obviously more communicative."

The driver, a dark-haired guy in a suit jacket and button-down shirt does this single grunt/laugh. I can't tell what the joke is.

Howard is scrolling through her phone.

That's something I really miss, my phone. I could know the date, where I'm at, any news. I'm adrift right now.

The exit we take says, New Appling. Never heard of it.

"We are facilitating a reunion between Navarro here and her alien friend," Baldy is explaining, "Try to engage in conversation. Keep them talking. Keep it light and friendly. Leave the car running, dashcam on."

We made our way to a farm. Barn, silos, fields, and a cute little white farmhouse.

Behind the barn is where we found the shuttlecraft.

My body is tense with excitement. I really can't wait to see Lu. It's weird because he's a terrifying, monstrous, murderous alien. But this whole time I've been detained, I've felt so alone like it's me against these agents. Even before that, dealing with all of the harassment and stalking, my friends all distanced themselves from me and my drama. My family hasn't really been supportive of me or really even close with me since I dropped out of college. In contrast, Lu was one hundred percent on my side. He murdered those two guys to defend me. He kept me safely away from all of the violence that went down on that ship. Maybe it's crazy. I know it's crazy. The thing is that I've been on guard and on my own for years now. It's so draining. But looking back at how protectively Lu treated me, it's like a fleece blanket, warm and comforting when the rest of the time I'm bare and chilled.

So, anyway, I'm pumped about seeing him again.

As the door appears on the side of the shuttle, Baldie hands me my translation device and I hook it onto my ear. It does this squeezing pulse thing, the same thing it did the first time.

And now there's a ramp leading down from the shuttle and a

person is on the ramp and—

It's not Lu.

It's not even an alien at all. It's a human woman. Just a regular woman. I mean she's cute, with long curly dark hair and a curvy hour-glass figure. She is wearing what looks like a long, bright red scarf wrapped all around her body.

"*Ohmygawd!*" She squeals and runs down the ramp, past Baldie, Howard, and the other agent, right toward me.

"I knew I recognized you!" She grabs my hand that's not holding Peach in hers and kind of jumps up and down.

I'm startled and confused, but I can't help but laugh at this strange lady's exuberance.

"Glory!"

Ah, that's what she's yelling about.

"GloryinGaming!"

That's my handle. I know. Cringe.

"I follow you on YouTube and TikTok and the interviews—"

She stops and visibly struggles to calm herself.

"Okay, okay. I'm done fan-girling. I promise. It's just—" She smooths out the skirt on her scarf/dress and takes a deep breath. "Anyway, Lu told me all about you and I saw the footage, but I didn't realize you were—" She gestures up and down my whole body. "You!"

I laugh at her because she's just too much.

"Anyway, I wanted to come get you because I saw those guys who tried to kidnap you. In Lu's neural implant footage. And then, I thought that the government," she waves a hand toward the agents who are all just silently observing, "might be treating you some kind of way. And Lu was…"

She pauses and looks at me obviously trying to come up with the right words.

"Would you like to come stay on the homeship with Lu and me and two other aliens? I swear, they're nice guys. And there's plenty of room." She smiles warmly at me. She has grabbed my hand again and gives it an encouraging squeeze.

This is a no-brainer. I never want to go back to that facility in my life. And I can't trust that Baldie is going to keep his word and let me go free when this is all over. Why should he?

"Yes, okay," I agree.

She lets out an excited squeal then says, "Great! I'm so happy! I mean, listen, I love the guys. But they're aliens. Like alien, aliens. It'll be so nice to have another human on board!"

"Okay, well, I'm Gloria." I would hold out my hand to shake, but she's already holding it, so I just squeeze. "This is Princess Peach."

"Oh, how cute! I'm Mandy by the way."

"Excuse me," Baldie says from behind me. "We are here to speak to—"

"Yeah, yeah, yeah," as Mandy interrupts him she's reaching behind her back.

I tense up for a second, like, does she have a weapon? But no, it's a device. Like an iPad, but oval-shaped and the screen dips in a little bit. She reaches around me and hands it to Baldie.

"That's the schematics. Listen, I was going to get a small planetary defense system, but then I thought about all of the satellites and rockets and SpaceX and everything. And I thought, you know what? We need to go bigger. So I got a multi-planet-ary defense system! It encompasses the whole Solar System, isn't that amazing?" Mandy takes a breath and looks at Baldie expect-antly.

"I, um—" He looks down at the alien device in his hand, "Yes, amazing."

"Well, just know that anything you guys send past the Kuiper Belt is going to get dusted. Sorry about that, but you're not doing anything out there anyway and it's just the price Earth has to pay for security, you know?"

"Uh, yeah. Yeah."

"And I have a professional overseeing the defense system. His name is Oh'Tech and if he has any issues or, God forbid, there's an incursion, he's going to call that tablet. don't lose it and don't break it."

"Yes. Of course."

"Okay." Mandy loops an arm through mine and starts leading me to the shuttle. "Let's go."

"Wait, just a moment," Howard says in her baby-doll voice.

"Oh, right." Baldie straightens his jacket. "Howard here would like to accompany Gloria and visit your ship."

I freeze. This is awful. Howard is going to follow me onto a spaceship? Will I ever be free of this awful woman?

"Why?" Mandy asks.

Howard answers, "To see Gloria settled and make sure she's safe—"

"No, thanks." I cut her off.

Mandy looks at the agents who are looking from each other to her and then back. Bald Guy says, "Perhaps you should check with the, well, whoever is in charge of your ship?"

"To ask if they want another human woman?" Mandy laughs good-naturedly. "It's my ship. So, no thanks. Jeez, you guys thought this was a Mars Needs Women situation?"

I don't know what she means, but it makes Baldie blush.

She continues leading me up the ramp to the shuttle and says over her shoulder, "We'll call that tablet, alright? And you'll see that Gloria is really okay and happy."

"But—"

"Sorry! Gotta go!" she yells as we step inside the shuttle.

The door seals shut.

I didn't see her push a button or anything. It just closes and then the shuttle is already moving.

I look around for a seat and don't see any, just this cavernous space.

"Yeah, there's no seats. Homeworlder shuttles don't have any. But don't worry, it won't be that rough." She pulls me toward the back of the shuttle and places my hand on a bar along the wall. "Here, hold this."

There is some turbulence and I'm white-knuckling the bar as Mandy continues to chat.

"So that went really well! I thought I was going to have to do some tense negations or deal with some sort of threats or hostage taking or something."

"Yeah," I answer, my voice a little breathless. "It went well."

"I told the guys that it had to be me that came and got you because I just felt like the aliens would be more likely to run into trouble, you know? Like they might get violent. The agents, not the aliens. Well, maybe the aliens, too."

I nod.

"I think that's why it went so well. Like, they were expecting some weird, unknown alien to come out of the shuttle, but instead it's little ole me. It threw off all their plans, I bet."

I nod again. I'm feeling a little queasy. Might be motion sickness or maybe just stress.

"So, you wanted to come with me, right? Those government people didn't pressure you into it?" she asks.

"Oh, I wanted to. Otherwise, they would have detained me in their awful facility for the rest of my life."

"Oh, no, was it awful?"

I nod. "They were keeping me in a kind of solitary confinement. It was driving me nuts."

"That's so wrong."

She does a kind of side hug thing and I tear up a little bit. It's nice to talk with someone who isn't an agent. Someone who has empathy and basic human kindness.

"So, I bet you were expecting to see Lu?" she asks.

I nod. "They said an extra-terrestrial wanted to meet with me. He's the only alien I know so—"

"And you looked pretty excited to see him. Before I walked onto the ramp."

I blush, but I don't know why I'm embarrassed. "Well, I know this sounds crazy because he's a terrifying alien. But we had been through a lot of stuff together. He murdered two guys who were trying to kidnap me. And he kept me safe and with him on that spaceship. I guess I have a case of hero worship where he's concerned."

"Really?"

"Yeah, I really was excited to see him again."

She laughs and jokes, "Well, I must have been a disappoint-ment then."

I shake my head.

She holds up a palm. "Kidding. I'm sure we'll see him as soon as we dock. The guys are probably waiting right outside the shut-tle bay."

As she's speaking, I hear a familiar *schlepp* then click. We're already docking to the ship.

CHAPTER FIFTEEN

—GLORIA—

Lu isn't waiting when we get off the shuttle. For a moment I thought he was, but it was another, smaller tentacled alien. They look very similar, but this one is definitely a different person. As soon as we leave the shuttle, a tentacle snakes tightly around Mandy's waist.

I jump back in surprise, but she just pats the tentacle-like it belongs there and introduces me to this new alien.

"Gloria, this is Seven. Seven, this is Gloria. She's going to be staying here with us."

"Greetings, Gloria." Seven does a smooth bow. "I am glad you are here."

"Oh? Why?" I ask. Not to be rude, but I am a little nervous about these aliens and their intentions.

"Tiny was adamant that you should. She would have been very disappointed if you had declined to visit."

The translator does a weird thing when he says Tiny. It translates the word, but my understanding quickly changes it to Mandy's name. Weird.

"They named me Tiny before English was integrated into the translation matrix. now Mandy means Tiny and Tiny means Mandy," she explains.

That's funny, especially because Mandy is more on the curvy/full-figured end of the spectrum. But I guess compared to these tentacle aliens, she is tiny.

"Where's Lu and Ken?" she asks.

"Ken is organizing all of the Earth things you had transported earlier. I do not know where Lu is."

"Ugh! Ken has no idea what that stuff is. How does he plan to organize things he knows nothing about?"

"I did not ask. We cannot use our shuttles as storage though. I allowed him to unload it."

"Fine. I'll just sort it out later." She waves her hand around dismissively. "Let's give Gloria a tour."

They show me all around. There's a cafeteria, a storage bay, a shuttle bay, and a whole bunch of private quarters, most of them unoccupied. And there's a swimming pod. It has a circle in the floor and that's the entrance. Apparently, you dive into that circle, swim down, around, and up through a tunnel, and eventually find a giant spherical space filled with water. It's useless for us humans because there are no surface or air pockets to catch a breath. Homeworlder aliens can breathe underwater. It's great fun for them.

There are great murals all over this ship. All earth/human stuff like Disney characters and pinup girls. I ask Mandy about it, and she says, "Oh, yeah. I'll tell you all about Earth-Human Art tomorrow. It's a funny story, but a long one."

I bet. I thought Mandy was joking when she told those agents that the ship was hers, but it seems true. She's decorated the whole thing and is explaining everything to me with a proprietary air. I wonder how she came to be in charge of this ship when it's obviously designed for the tentacled Homeworlders?

"This is the medbay," Mandy says as we turn a corner, and a door opens. "That's the regen tank," she waves toward a huge blue tank, "and here is where you can come and get scanned if you want. It's painless, and a full physical in under a minute."

"Nice." I compliment. This is such a weird situation. I'm complimenting this woman's spaceship's med-bay. My life just keeps getting crazier.

We tour the whole ship, but we don't bump into Lu. Mandy introduces Ken when we find him in the storage bay. He's sorting out a whole bunch of stuff. It looks like someone raided at least three different department stores and stuffed a shuttle full of everything that could fit. Clothes, dishes, bedding, toys, and everything else. Why does Mandy need all of this stuff on a spaceship? She already showed me the replicators. There is a large industrial one for printing bigger things and a smaller one that seems to be just for food. Strange that she went on a shopping spree when she could make anything she wants out of thin air.

Ken holds out a monstrously clawed hand and says, "I am happy to meet you—"

"Gloria," Mandy supplies.

"Gloria." Ken says, looking pleased with himself as he shakes my hand. All of the other words were in a hiccupy alien language, but my name was carefully pronounced.

"Would you like to supply Gloria with some of these nesting materials?" He uses a tentacle gesture toward a pile of sheets, blankets, and pillows. "Or had you planned to replicate something for her?"

"Oh, I already took care of all that," Mandy answers. "All of this stuff is for trade."

All of his tentacles that had been moving around this whole time still. "For trade you say?"

Mandy nods emphatically. "Yes. You know how everyone is going nuts about Earth-Human stuff? I thought I'd grab up a bunch of things—"

"Tiny, it is Earth-Human art that is valuable. Not these," he holds up a monster high doll in a tentacle and waves it around, "other things."

"What makes you think these things don't have artistic value?"

Ken doesn't answer.

"Art is whatever people say it is. And everyone thinks anything to do with humans is inherently artistic. Sal sold all of those appliances, didn't he?"

All of Ken's tentacles do a quick bob at the same time as he says, "You are correct. We can probably trade these items on artistic merits."

He holds the doll closer to his face, examining it. "Sal would surely be interested."

"Why are you unhappy about it?" Mandy asks. I wasn't going to say anything, but Ken does look unhappy about trading this stuff. His coloring has gotten darker. I had noticed with Lu that his color would suddenly darken when he's upset.

Ken's tentacles all do a quick bob then a small shake and he says, "I am not unhappy about trading these items. I have been organizing and placing them in the personal use area," he waves a tentacle toward the near wall that has a bunch of shelves and cubbies, then explains, "Now I need to move all of it to the area for trade items." He waves the tentacle toward the opposite wall where large containers are stacked in neat rows.

"Oh, no, you don't have to do any of that. I'll sort it out tomorrow," Mandy tells him.

He waves his tentacles around again. This guy really likes to gesture with those tentacles. He just keeps his arms folded across his chest for the most part.

"No, I will do it. I was just frustrated for a moment that I had not done it right in the first place." Ken's color does seem to be lightening. "I will sort this out."

"Well, thanks. I really appreciate it, Ken. You're the best." Mandy smiles at the tentacled alien as she delivers this praise and he smiles back, baring sharp fangs as his skin takes on a lavender tone.

"Ken's acting weird," Mandy informs me in the hallway after we leave the storage bay.

I shrug because this is the first time I've met him. I don't know what weird is when it comes to him.

"Where's Lu? I expected to see him by now."

At first, I think she's asking me, but Seven answers from behind her.

"He is hiding. He has disabled the tracking function of his implant."

I had kind of forgotten that Seven was following behind us. How could I have stopped noticing this monstrous tentacled alien looming over us the whole time?

"Why would he hide from us though?" Mandy asks.

Nobody has an answer.

Could it be that Lu is hiding from me? It can't be a coincidence that the same day I come aboard, he disappears.

"Okay, here's your room."

We've stopped in front of a door panel that opens automatically. There's a platform bed and a low table. The bed has a bunch of thin brightly colored blankets and pillows. It looks very fluffy and comfortable. The walls are painted kind of—abstractly? Like there are four main colors, white, light gray, dark gray, and sea-blue, and they overlap each other in a few different places around the room. And where the colors come together it's blended in a frothy kind of way like they are waves crashing onto each other. It's a very nice, calming effect. After spending all that time in stark-white boring surroundings, I appreciate this decor.

"Do you like it?" Mandy blurts out impatiently. She's been waiting for me to say something, I guess.

"Yes. It's lovely. I really like it," I assure her. She beams with pride and smiles up at Seven, who just looks pleased that she's happy.

"What's this, though?" I ask pointing at a raised rectangle on the floor.

"Oh, that's for Your dog. If you can get her to use it, her waste will just disappear," she explains.

"Disappear?"

She nods. "Yeah, I've had it explained to me twice, but I still don't understand how it works. Something about anti-matter. But it really does work. Guaranteed."

That sounds kind of dangerous, but I guess I just need to trust that the things on this spaceship are safe.

"Okay."

I shift Peach from one arm to another. She has been very well-behaved today, all things considered.

"Across the way, there is a bathroom. I can show you how to use the laser-shower tomorrow. And down there on the right is mine and Seven's room." She points as she talks.

"Yours and Seven's?" I ask. There has been a bit of a couple vibe going on, but I had thought that maybe these aliens are just very touchy-feely, and Mandy is nice about it? Lu grabbed and touched me a few times, it could just be an alien thing?

But no. This confirms that they are together like that.

"Yeah, mine and Seven's and our kids'." Mandy straightens her shoulders and seems to kind of square off with me as she says this. Like she's bracing herself for something.

"Your kids?" I ask. This is the first time anybody has mentioned anything about kids on this ship.

"Yes."

"Okay, well I'm kind of beat. I'll just meet the kids tomorrow."

Mandy smiles and relaxes her shoulders, but Seven growls at me.

"Gawd, Seven, cut it out!" Mandy admonishes him, then turns to me. "Of course, you can meet the babies!" She tells me happily.

Seven does not look happy.

Mandy waves as she steps out the door. "Sleep well! I'm so glad you're here!"

After the door closes behind them, I set Peach down on the anti-matter pet-pad. She circles once and immediately gets down to business. I have never in my life been so interested in dog poo, but I watch intently waiting for it to disappear. And it does. It just blinks out of existence. It's just gone.

Crazy.

So, there are few weird things going on. Mandy and Seven are together-together. It's weird. They shouldn't be compatible with each other biologically. They definitely shouldn't have babies. Multiple babies, like what the hell?

This is all impossible. And it's also not really my business.

And what's going on with Lu? Why would he be hiding and avoiding me? That kind of blows. Here I was thinking that he was behind all this and had come back for me, that I had this connection with an alien who would swoop in like a superhero to save the day. How many people have alien BFFs after all?

But in reality, he doesn't even want to see me. I was actually rescued by this strange woman who wants human company.

This is still a good situation though. Much better than the facility I had been detained at. Better even than my life before all this alien stuff because internet stalkers can't find me here, can they? I can let go of that stress for a while.

And look at this room. Mandy obviously went through a lot of trouble to make me feel welcome. It's nice.

I should figure out some work to do, some way to contribute around here so that I'm not a burden. Hopefully, I can stay for a while. I don't really know how to contribute though.

Snuggling under the covers with Peach, I let go of all these questions and worries and fall into the deepest most restful sleep I've had in years.

CHAPTER SIXTEEN

—LU—

Following a few paces behind Gloria, I am careful to remain unobtrusive and quiet. It has become a joke to others on this ship that I refuse to be in the same room as Gloria. I will not interact with her. She brings out the absolute worst in me. There is a part of me that has always been locked away, but in her presence, a key is turned, and I am a possessive, violent male. Willing to do murder on her behalf, take on a whole ship-full of drones, align myself with a monstrous Arana-Vora just for the chance to save her, to avenge her. She never asked me to do these things, but I would do more. There is a dissatisfaction to me now, darkly waiting to do battle on her behalf. I am no longer the male I was, but perhaps if I can avoid her and go about my tasks as if I am not changed—

But I cannot keep myself from following her now. It is embarrassing, but I have stalked her this way at least fifteen times since she has come to live with us. She is not overly loud the way Tiny is, but humans have a certain obliviousness to their surroundings and one can hear them coming before they enter a room. And when they do enter, they will not always look around. They just assume their surroundings are safe, that no one is stalking them.

Gloria is especially oblivious right now because she has been drinking booze with Mandy. They had been having a "girls' night" which is when human women drink inebriating substances, talk loudly, and laugh a lot. Seven, Ken, and I had watched anxiously from a security alcove as they consumed serving after serving of Urglassi wine. Humans have very robust biologies. Knock-out gas does not work on them, and Mandy has even woken up while immersed in regen goop. But wine works exactly as prescribed on these delicate little humans.

"Werk werk werk werk werk..." She's singing this song that is not translating at all as she teeters down the hall.

Seven had rushed Mandy away from their "girls' night" because some kind of alarm had gone off in their room. Perhaps one of their spawn was trying to escape the tank? At such an early point in their development, Homeworlder young are nowhere near close to independence. They must remain in a tank of nutrient-rich water until they mature. What of their human genetics though? Humans develop at a different pace and a different way—

"Werk werk w—" Gloria suddenly spins around, dancing as she is singing, and loses her footing.

One of my tentacles snakes out and wraps around her, cushioning her before she hits the floor.

"Oh," she says, smiling crookedly at me. "There you are."

I lift her into my upper arms, holding her close as I continue toward her quarters.

"You've been avoiding me," she accuses.

She has not protested, it must be allowable for me to hold her this way. Her scent is divine, though tinged with Urglassi wine. She is soft, warm, and happy right now, not shocked or tense at my handling. Is it inebriation that is making her so relaxed in my company and in my embrace? With her in this state, this is the best way to get her safely to her quarters.

I move slowly to make this last.

"You're big," she comments then pats me on the chest.

I do not respond, but I do find myself carefully detangling her mane as I move through the corridors. She does not seem to notice, and it takes all of my concentration not to purr in her ear. Her mane is soft and smells good.

"So, how does it work?" She has angled her head back to look up at me.

"How does what work?" I ask.

"Mandy and Seven. They're together. They have babies. Did they do it? Is it the same as when humans do it?"

Obviously, the *it* she is referring to is breeding. Do Tiny and Seven breed in the same manner as humans? I have never watched humans breed. But I know they have two sexes: a breeding type and an insemination type. That's already very different from Homeworlders who only have one sex which is an implantation type. Or is she only referring to the act itself?

Finally, I reply with, "There is a video log. You could see for yourself."

That should answer her curiosity.

She jerks in my arms, startled, and I tighten my hold to keep her from falling.

"Mandy and Seven made a sex tape?"

The translation matrix is having difficulty with the word tape. Cleary, she is not referring to an adhesive strip. Tape seems to be another word for video.

"There is a security feed that runs continuously. They mated in the shuttle-bay and the record is saved in the video log that you can watch in one of the security alcoves."

She is twisting her head around looking all around the corridor. I cannot tell what she is looking for, but I hold her securely while she does it.

At length, she says, "Um, I don't think Mandy wants me to watch that."

"Then she should not have mated with Seven in the shuttle bay. They could have moved to a private room if they were concerned. Or deleted the footage."

"Does Mandy even know about the footage?" She sounds accusing. I cannot know what she thinks I have done, but she is upset with me about something.

"She knows. I have seen a log of her watching it, she definitely knows about it," I explain.

84

"You just sit around watching videos of Mandy? What are you stalking her?"

Gloria scents very strongly of alarm and accusation right now. It is not pleasant.

"The security logs are available for anybody to review. If you do something in a public area of this ship, it is recorded and logged. It is not private. It is not a violation to review the log."

She is no longer happy with me holding her and we have reached her quarters, I carefully set her on her own two feet. She is still a little wobbly.

She stares up at me, hands in little fists on her hips, eyes ablaze with this mysterious accusation. I get the impression that even though she is head and shoulders shorter than me, she is attempting to look down her nose at me.

"Does Seven know that you're obsessed with Mandy?"

"No. Because I am not."

Her face is a storm cloud. Deeply brown eyes sparkling, eyebrows drawn together. She is adorable, like if a little woodland creature were to hop out at you and squeak to berate you for some offense.

"Why are you smiling?" she asks, waving a hand toward my face.

"You are adorable," I tell her in honesty.

Now the hand is a fist, and she is still waving it at me. As though to strike me. This is the cutest thing I have ever seen in my life. Her scent still conveys irritation, but also pleasure. My female enjoys compliments, does she?

"Don't try and flirt with me!"

"Is that what this is? Flirting?"

She shakes her head vehemently. "No."

"So, if I tell you that you are gorgeous—" there's that pleased scent again, "that you smell divine. That it is you that I obsess over. You and your scent and your softness and your beauty—" She is trying to maintain her indignation, but she is so pleased. I can smell it. "This is flirting?"

"You—you're messing with me!" she accuses.

"I am sincere."

"But you've been avoiding me."

"I—"

"You know what? I can't deal with this." She makes a gesture at me. "It's too weird. I just can't. I'm going to bed."

With that, she storms into her room and the door closes behind her.

I am left to wonder, what is it that's too weird? Me? Us?

She may have a point.

CHAPTER SEVENTEEN
—GLORIA—

Mandy is always doing at least five things at once. Like now, for instance, she is working on a mural. It's a really crazy take on Dante's Inferno. She's got the layers of hell, right? But instead of it being all creepy and scary and torturous, it's full of cute stuff. Minions, Baby Yoda, puppies, kittens, penguins, all of the demons and devils are unbearably cute with tiny little horns, wings, and tails. All of the lost souls are being prodded along by pitch-fork-wielding cuties. And in the center of it all, on a throne of bones and skulls is Hello Kitty. It's all done in bright, vibrant colors that remind me of Lisa Frank trapper-keepers (no, I'm not old enough to have used a trapper-keeper, but I found a crate of them at a thrift store once).

As she's painting this mural, she is organizing her financial empire. Apparently, she stumbled across a stash of really valuable credits. Whenever these aliens talk about credits, I think they mean imaginary money. Like how paychecks would go into my account, and I would pay for stuff with my card without ever touching any physical money. The kind of currency that never actually, physically exists. But Mandy's credits are a rare and valuable physical currency, and she has a whole ton of them. On top of that, she really does own this ship. All three aliens were arrested at some point and when Mandy tried to get them back, the alien government gave her the ship that had been seized from Ken, Lu, and Seven. Legally, not physically. Mandy was stranded on the ship the whole time. It's really dumb because Mandy can't operate the ship because she doesn't have an implant and she won't get one.

Anyway, Mandy is loaded, and she wants to use all that money to protect Earth from Seereechees and track down and rescue enslaved/abducted humans.

So that's something else she's always doing, following leads to try and find humans.

But right now she's brainstorming how to make more credits.

"Did you know that none of these alien planets are nearly as populated as Earth?" she asks me as she paints tiny flames dancing around a horned minion.

I shake my head.

"Well, the average is about a hundred thousand sentients on any inhabited planet. And a lot of them are far fewer. Most of them have issues with fertility, which keeps their populations low. And every now and then a war will break out that makes it worse."

Sipping an electrolyte drink, I'm lounging on a beanbag near Mandy as she works and thinks. She says that Ken usually fills this role, but he's acting weird lately, so I volunteered to keep her company, chat, and bounce ideas around. She's like a whirlwind of talk and activity and I just nod along. I'm paying attention, but I don't really have much to add.

"I don't think they've really invented modern banking. Like, interest, bonds, investing and all that. They just trade and pay each other and the money just sits there. I'm sure loans are made, but not like they are on earth."

"So, what," I ask, "are you going to open an intergalactic bank?"

"I think so."

"But do you know anything about starting up a bank?"

"Nope, but I'm a learn as I go type."

I wish I had her confidence. Imagine just deciding to start something and never even considering that you might not be good at it?

She hums as she continues painting, then says, "I need to set up a human sanctuary. Somewhere for people to recover from slavery and abduction and decide if they really want to go back to Earth."

"I sure don't," I tell her. "I bet every single person who's returned to Earth is being detained by one government agency or another."

"I think you're right."

She hums for a little bit as she works. This painting looks done to me, but she just keeps going.

"So, Seven says that I could just buy a whole planet or a moon with the credit coins, to set up a reserve. It would be a bad idea to try to set it up on a planet owned by someone else. But then I'd be pretty much wiped out financially."

"Can you terraform a planet? Like one that can't support life yet?"

"Yeah, that might be cheaper. Like a fixer-upper planet." She grins at me.

"Well, I think you could get one for free to terraform. Or maybe install some kind of bio-dome," I suggest slowly, thinking it through. "Then you'd only have to pay for the process of making it livable and not the planet itself."

"Oh?"

"Yeah, nobody owns Mars, do they? And you already have that defense system set up protecting the whole solar system. And I think that there are a few moons around Jupiter you could work with." I'm really warming to this idea. I like to think of Mandy claiming all this real estate in our solar system. Not USA, Russia, EU, but Mandy of Earth and her intergalactic refugees just taking up residence.

"That's true! I think this is going to work out for real, Gloria. But what I really need are a few different streams of income. If I just continue spending, eventually I'm going to run out of credits."

"So, banking."

"Yes, but I'm going to start really small and be very subtle about it. Also, I need to keep a monopoly on Earth Art and keep fueling that demand."

I shake my head at her. "You need to slow your roll just a little bit, hon. You can't own all art that every human makes."

"No, but now that I have the Solar-system closed off, I can control distribution. And if I rescue any artistically inclined humans, I'll be the one showing them the ropes if they want in on this Earth-Human-Art craze."

I laugh at her. "This is starting to sound less like a charitable enterprise and more like an evil capitalist empire."

She shrugs. "You know, I think in order for the charitable part to succeed, the capitalist part has to work too."

I don't really know if that's true. I'm kind of worried about introducing Earth-style banking and investing to an unsuspecting universe. Just because something is a fact of life on Earth doesn't necessarily mean that it needs to spread.

"So, um, change of subject." She glances at me, and I nod for her to continue.

"You know that there is video and audio surveillance in public areas of this ship," she says. It's not a question.

"Yeah," I agree.

"Well, this morning I reviewed the footage from last night because I wanted to check that you made it back to your room."

"Okay."

"I was worried because I'd just left you alone and you were kind of drunk, you know?"

I nod.

"So, I heard your conversation with Lu."

This is embarrassing. She heard me accuse Lu of being obsessed with her. I must have sounded like some crazed, jealous girlfriend. And Lu isn't my boyfriend. He's an alien, for Chrissake!

"There's something I think you should know, and I didn't bring it up before you came aboard because I didn't want to scare you off. And after that there was never a good time."

Well, that's not ominous at all.

She looks at me for a moment then speaks, "Homeworlders have a really bad reputation. A long time ago, when they first left their own planet, they would kidnap other aliens, implant them with eggs, and hold them hostage until the eggs matured. That's how they reproduced in those days, and it pissed everybody else in the universe off. Two wars were fought about it and Homeworld was poisoned and made unlivable, so all of the Homeworlders had to relocate to a different planet."

"Oh, wow." What else is there to say to something like that?

"Yeah, and now all babies on Homeworld Two are grown in tanks. Nobody reproduces in a regular way on that planet. It's illegal. A whole lot of things are illegal. There aren't any families, nobody has parents—"

I hold up a hand to interrupt. "So the way they reproduce is so predatory and offensive to the rest of the universe that it's now illegal?"

She nods and says, "Yeah. And they are so dumb about it because instead of learning from other species how to have relationships with consent and reciprocity, leaders on Homeworld were like 'If we can't kidnap and coerce sex partners then no sex ever again for any of us!'"

She does a weird hiccupy impression, imitating Homeworlder speech that's just goofy and not at all accurate. It makes me giggle.

She continues to explain, "Okay, the point of all this is that Homeworld Two is very isolated. And even Homeworlders like Seven, Lu, and Ken who were able to leave the planet are isolated because it's illegal and socially taboo for them to live with anyone who isn't a Homeworlder. The whole universe still remembers the wars and why they happened. Homeworlders aren't well thought of."

I nod because that makes sense.

"I'm telling you all this," she continues, "so that you'll understand that Lu doesn't know anything about flirting, or relationships, or anything like that. He doesn't know how to play the kind of games that humans play about sex and relationships, you know what I mean?"

I slowly nod as all of this information coalesces in my brain, but then I point out, "But he has been avoiding me ever since I came on the ship. Then he tells me he's obsessed with me. And then he goes right back to avoiding me this morning."

"Yeah, well I think he has an explanation for it and it's not that he's playing games. You should let him explain."

Mandy is a steamroller. On top of everything else she's working on and thinking through, she's concerning herself with mine and Lu's conversations as if she has any business—

"And you might want to review the security logs and check what Lu has been doing while he's avoiding you."

I shake my head. "What's with you all telling me to watch security logs? I'm not the type to spy on people—"

"Ugh." She tosses her paint-brush-like tool into the box that floats beside her when she's painting. Then she taps the side of it, and it closes and floats to the ground. "Come on. This way."

Usually, I like Mandy, but right now she's getting on my nerves with her pushiness and nosiness. I follow her anyway.

When we get to the security alcove, Mandy gets a small tablet out of one of the folds of her wrap-skirt. The alcove is meant to interact with the neural implants the aliens have but has a work-around with the tablet. She taps at the tablet for a second and then uses voice commands to bring up the log from last night.

I'm in this video, and I'm teetering drunkenly down the hallway, singing a Rihanna song.

"Watch," Mandy tells me.

Me in the video spins around and almost falls, but Lu appears out of nowhere and catches me.

"Data," Mandy says (she has named the security AI Data.) "Switch to thermal mode, rewind three minutes, then play."

It switches over to a kind of infrared vision and I can see now that Lu was following me very closely the whole time.

"That creepy alien!"

"Yeah and look at this." She rewinds further and we watch Lu follow me around ten more times.

"It seems to me," she opines as we watch Lu sneaking behind me, "that he is obsessed with you, just like he said. But he's trying to give you space for some reason."

This should be bad news, but I can't help a frisson of warmth that moves through me. He's not dangerous to me. After everything that's happened with him, I know that he's most dangerous when he's protecting me from something. The idea that he's following me around makes me feel—good? Protected?

I don't know what Mandy expects me to do with this information though.

CHAPTER EIGHTEEN

—GLORIA—

After Mandy's little lesson, I know how to track down Lu now and I find him in the swimming pod. There is only one way out of it and that is the hole in the floor. The alien guys dive in there and it's a twisty turning tunnel to the big, spherical pod that they swim around in. Ken explained to me that it needs to be a pod and can't be a human-style pool because if something were to happen with the gravity on this ship, we need all that water to stay where it's at. If it was a pool, the water could just float up and away, messing up other parts of the ship.

So it's just a room with a hole in the floor and I'm waiting here for Lu to come out. Waiting and waiting. The longer I wait, the more determined I am.

I sit against the wall and rest my head on my knees. I keep my knees together and sit as demurely as I can because I don't want his first sight when he comes out to be right up my skirt. I've found I like Mandy's style of wrapping a length of cloth around my hips and tying it off for a sarong type of skirt. These and a few T-shirts Mandy gave me from her department store stash make for a very comfortable wardrobe.

This waiting in total silence is giving me lots of time to think.

If Lu is avoiding me, why am I here trying to force something? What do I even want to talk with him about?

I'd like to gain an understanding of what has scared him off.

Why he works so hard to avoid me?

But the real question is, why do I care?

I don't really know why. I know what Mandy thinks though. She has been playing matchmaker this whole time.

But honestly, I'm not going to date an alien. I'm a human woman and I only date humans. End of. He has tentacles, for goodness sake.

My mind briefly flashes to some of the stranger hentai I've seen. Listen, I'm not a perv, but I have been on the internet, so I know about weird porn. It's awkward and disturbing, not hot at all.

But other people must like it otherwise there wouldn't be as much interest in it. Mandy obviously doesn't object to weird alien anatomy.

And who am I kidding with a "humans only" dating policy? I've decided not to go back to Earth, ever. I'm going to make a life for myself out here in space. Socializing with aliens is part of that. There aren't a lot of humans to choose from out here. If I couldn't make a relationship work with humans back on Earth, why hold on to the notion out here. Am I really going to give up on relationships and sex? Forever?

That's something to think about, but it's not reason enough to fall into Mandy's match-making trap.

Lost in thought, staring at the floor, I almost miss the small splashing sound of Lu getting out of the pool. When I jerk my head up, I catch a glimpse of him. But then he quickly camouflages. I can still make out his shape, but it's hard. If I didn't already know he was there—

"You're being ridiculous," I tell him.

His color quickly washes out to a dark gray as he says, "I am being considerate."

"How? Where I come from, it's rude to ignore people."

"I never ignore you."

Flashing through my thoughts are the videos of him following me. He's right, ignore is the wrong word. Why does the reminder of him stalking me make me feel—warm?

"This pleases you?"

I wave off that question as I stand and ask my own, "Okay, you don't really ignore me, but you are avoiding me. How's that considerate?"

"My form," he gestures at his lower body with all of those tentacles, "is offensive to you. And so is my touch. I keep myself away from you and out of sight to spare you."

"That's not true at all! Why would you think that?"

"I could smell your alarm. When we were abducted, every time we touched for any reason, you were startled and offended."

I shake my head. "That's just not true."

"Your pheromones do not lie. I could smell your stress responses, the scent saturated the whole enclosure."

"I was being held captive! And you were grabbing at me!"

I'm getting worked up. I try to calm down just a smidge then ask, "What about last night? How did I smell when you carried me to my room?

"Inebriated." He grins when he answers.

The whole time we've been talking, the color of his skin has been lightening from dark, storm cloud gray to a light shimmery color. Just now, when I mentioned him carrying me, his upper chest warmed to a subtle pink. Pink means happy, doesn't it? I think Mandy told me it does.

"So let's see if I'm understanding you." I step over a couple tentacles and stand nearer to him looking up into his weird yellow eyes. "You want to be near me, but you don't like my smell when you've touched me in the past and now you're avoiding me."

"No, you—"

"How do I smell now?"

"What?"

"I'm near you." I gesture toward my feet where two tentacles are winding around my ankles. "You're touching me. How do I feel about it? Can you tell?"

"You—" He shakes his head as though in a daze. "You smell

annoyed. And pleased." He lowers himself, adjusting his height by spreading his tentacles across the floor and winding them around each other. Leaning over me, he takes an audible sniff of my hair. The tentacles winding up my calves tighten. "You smell excited."

My cheeks warm and I shrug then say, "I wouldn't go that far."

"If you enjoy my touch, why did you slap me and rebuke me when I touched you before?"

I'm distracted by how his tentacles are winding up my legs. The undersides are textured and have two rows of cups that kind of stick then unstick as they move. It feels like I'm being stroked and licked and squeezed all at the same time and it's overwhelming my senses.

You know how earlier I thought I would never be into an alien at all? I was mistaken. Maybe I'm some sort of perv, but it's occurred to me that the little cups that are moving against my inner thigh right now could move higher and be put to better use

—

"Gloria."

"Huh?" I've lost the thread of our conversation. The way he's looming over me—

Lifting my arms to run my hands over his shoulders, I then twine them around his neck to pull him closer. I'm reveling in this. It's been a long time since I last felt this way, warm and needy and just plain turned on. It's crazy that it's this alien with his tentacles doing it.

I tilt my head back, inviting a kiss, but I immediately feel dumb because this is an alien. He probably doesn't know anything about kissing. Why am I even—

And then he purrs, I swear. He purrs like a giant house cat and makes this trilling sound that my translator lets me know is pleasure, just pure happiness. He rubs his cheek against mine and tucks his nose behind my ear where he draws a deep breath, clearly luxuriating in my scent.

He's just—he's so obvious!

Maybe I should be leery of him. He said he's obsessed with me, and he's been stalking me. But he's so unabashedly happy that I'm near him, allowing him to touch me.

Mandy was right. These aliens don't know how to play any games and he's not holding anything back. He's eagerly showing all of his feelings. From the pink glow of his skin to the rumbling purr, to that happy trilling sound, he's just—enraptured. And the reason he was staying away from me is because he thought I dislike him? That's just so—

There's something about such a big scary monster of an alien being so unsure and so sweet—it flips a switch in me. I forget everything except how this feels right now. And if he doesn't know how to kiss, I'm about to teach him.

Using the hold I have around his shoulders, I pull him down and he is putty in my hands offering no resistance at all. There's something thrilling about that. When I press my mouth to his though, he stills. Obviously shocked. For just a moment, I'm self-conscious, but then he purrs so strongly it vibrates my whole body where I'm plastered against him.

"For the love of—"

I spring apart from Lu, tripping over his tentacles. I almost fall, but he wraps one tentacle around my waist and steadies me.

It's Ken who's barged in on us and he's complaining, "What is it about humans and public mating displays? There are so many private rooms on this ship! Why—"

"Quiet." Lu maneuvers me behind him and faces off against Ken. "You will not speak to her that way."

"What way?" Ken asks, "And I am not speaking to just her."

"You have no right to censure us."

Ken rolls his eyes in a very human gesture he probably learned from Mandy. "Fine. Go ahead and mate in the swimming pod access room. Why would I mind?"

He scrunches all of his tentacles up at once in a Home-worlder gesture that I can't interpret and then, as Lu snarls at him, he leaps across the room and into the water. He swims out of sight before I could blink.

Huh. I didn't know they could jump at all, much less so far. The tentacles don't even have bones. How do they manage?

"Apologies," Lu says.

"No worries." I wave him off and shrug away from his grasp. He lets me go. "I'm going to go find Mandy. We're visiting a space station tonight."

"Risant Two." Lu supplies the name of the station.

"Yeah, exactly. So I'll, uh, see ya later," I say, then spin around and leave the room.

"See you later," I hear him say as I speed-walk away.

What the hell? I can't believe I was just caught making out with an alien.

CHAPTER NINETEEN

—GLORIA—

Mandy is in the cafeteria having lunch with Seven when I find her. I help myself to the food generator and sit down with them.

The noodle machine is pretty cool. At first, when I heard that noodles were all there was available to eat here, I could have cried. But I've found that they're printed out of this machine, and they can come in any texture, any flavor. The hard part is programming it. Luckily, Mandy brought all kinds of Earth food aboard just to program this machine. Nothing is ever exactly right like the fruits are dull, or the lemon flavor doesn't have any zing to it, stuff like that. The textures are always off a little bit too.

Mandy and I couldn't program it because we don't have implants, so we had the guys look, touch, and taste each food item and their neural implants programmed that information into the food machine. I have a suspicion that they don't have the same kind of taste buds as we do. But, anyway, it's fun to experiment and beats eating plain noodles every single day.

I order up some almost-orange chicken with fried rice-like noodles and take a seat with Mandy and Seven.

"So," I say between bites of food. "I just saw Ken jump across a room."

Mandy shakes her head. "He can't jump."

"I just saw him do it."

"It's kind of impossible with the way they're bodies are. Tentacles can't jump. Right Seven?"

Seven looks a little lost and says, "What do you mean by jump? I am getting multiple translations—"

Mandy stands up and walks around her seat then performs a few jumps.

"See how my feet left the ground? That's a jump."

She sits back down.

"We could jump under water," Seven says.

Mandy asks, "But could Ken have jumped across a room?"

Seven shakes his head.

"Well, I saw him do it. Review the logs if you don't believe me." As soon as the words leave my mouth I want to take them back.

"Okay, good idea."

I wave my hand and say, "Never mind."

"No, I'm curious now. I don't think you're lying, and I want to solve this mystery."

We continue to eat and chat about Ken.

Mandy mentions again that she feels like he's acting weird.

"He never hangs out while I'm painting anymore. And look, he used to have every single meal with us." She gestures around illustrating that Ken isn't in the room with us.

I glance at Seven, but he is looking down at his food. His tentacles are all moving with a slight jerk though. Like he's trying to hold them still, but not succeeding.

"Seven," I say, and he still doesn't look at me. "Do you know why Ken is acting weird?"

"I may have encouraged him to be more productive with his time."

Mandy is pissed. Her cheeks flush and her mouth has thinned into a hard line and she's holding her fork so tightly in her hand that it may break.

Seven continues, "I let him know that it is annoying for him to spend his free time following my mate around like a lost pet."

The fork snaps in half.

"I told him that he should be aware that he does not contribute any value to—"

Mandy stands then stomps to the reclamation bin and throws her dish and fork pieces inside with force causing them to clank together.

Seven has changed from his usual pink/purple color to a dark blue. "Dear One—"

"Gloria, please tell Seven I'm not talking to him."

Seven stills, his tentacles motionless. "What? Why—"

"I think he heard you," I interrupt.

I feel bad for Seven, but he was a total dick to Ken. He has to know that Mandy wouldn't want him interfering in her friendships like that. She's been really worried about Ken's strange behavior and Seven didn't say anything about it until now when I confronted him. What did he expect?

"Good." She studiously avoids looking in his direction. Linking her arm through mine she says with forced cheerfulness, "Let's go look at that security log."

Seven is hanging back, looking miserable as he follows us into the corridor.

"Gloria, please tell Seven that it's annoying when he follows us around like a lost pet."

I turn toward Seven. I'm not really going to repeat what she said. He's obviously heard, and he's stricken. He's as dark a color as I have ever seen on one of these guys, so blue he's nearly black. And all of his tentacles are still. Then he makes a trilling sound that is muffled and drawn out and just so very sad.

Mandy and I continue down the hallway and around the corner until he's out of sight.

"That was kinda harsh," I tell her.

She slumps her shoulders and sighs.

"I know. But it's not the first time he's pulled this sort of thing. He told me that it's instinctual guarding behavior that Homeworlders have toward hosts. But he's not an animal. He should be able to control himself. And anyway, he knows Ken isn't any kind of a threat. He's being an asshole at this point."

I nod because she's right. Seven shouldn't be so controlling and possessive. Like, it's okay for him to feel that way. But he shouldn't act that way.

"Why did Ken listen to him though?" I wonder aloud.

"I don't know. And to be honest, I don't think Seven's nonsense is the only explanation for it. Those two disagree and talk shit to each other all the time."

"Well, what's changed recently?" I ask her. "Besides me coming aboard?"

"Oh, well, they were arrested, had all of their credits and this ship confiscated, Lu and Ken were abducted by Seereechee slavers, then Lu was stranded on Earth all that time until he was abducted again—"

"Maybe you should give them back their ship," I suggest.

She purses her lips then asks, "What difference would that make? It's all of our home. It's not like I'm going to kick him off the ship."

"Well, it could be that Ken thinks of you as his boss now, ya know? Because he doesn't own anything and is basically living on charity, which Seven seems to have made clear to him. He probably feels kind of vulnerable and useless."

She's looking at me wide-eyed now. "You know, that makes sense. Here I was thinking that everyone understood that we're a family and everything is shared but—"

"Is that true though?" I cut in.

"What do you mean?"

"You have all the credits. You own the ship. You're making the plans and these aliens are your yes-men and I'm your personal assistant."

She looks a bit shocked.

"I'm not saying it's a bad thing," I reassure her. "Somebody has to be in charge. It might as well be you. I'm just pointing out that the relationship dynamic has changed between you and Ken because you're his boss now."

She grapples with this for a moment then asks, "But we're friends though, right, Gloria? You're not just—"

"Don't be silly."

"I'm serious."

"Don't be serious, either."

She laughs and I'm relieved because the tension that had strung between us evaporates.

"Okay." She nods. "Let's go check the log and then figure out how to give the ship back so these aliens aren't so completely at my mercy."

"Yes, Boss." She elbows me. "Ow, Boss."

When we review the footage on the security log, after Mandy teases me about making out with Lu, we see that Ken had reached out a tentacle and grabbed the edge of the pod entrance. He then used that hold to fling himself into it, pulling that tentacle taught then snapping it like a rubber band.

So he hadn't really jumped.

This investigation has piqued our curiosity though and now Mandy and I decide to go to the med-bay and figure out exactly how these aliens work, anatomically. Like, how do they hold themselves upright? Shouldn't they kind of flop around like an octopus does? What is anchoring their upper bodies to stand up straight?

It's quite a long lesson. And not as interesting as I thought it would be until we get a full anatomical map projected onto one wall. That's when I see something very interesting.

"Is that a dick?" I ask, pointing at what is too small to be a tentacle arm and a little too large to be a penis.

It looks vaguely shlong-like, but its ribbed, the base is a lot wider than the head and it seems to be kind of—bifurcated? Like, instead of the tiny slit on the head that human cocks have, the slit on this alien cock goes all the way from back to front splitting it in half. And instead of having a rounded cock-head, it's slightly pointed. And even though this picture doesn't show it, I get the impression that it can move independently, like a tentacle.

Mandy studies the rendering. "I don't know, it looks kind of weird, doesn't it?"

"Mandy, are you serious?"

"What?"

"You should know what it looks like."

She scrunches her face.

"You and Seven." I gesture at her and then at the map. "You know. He's your man—alien—Whatever. You've done it with him."

She's staring at me like I'm the crazy one.

"I didn't study it!"

"You didn't even look at it?"

She's blushing now.

"You had sex with an alien, and you didn't even check what he was working with?" I ask, shocked. "It could have had spikes or something! You could have been hurt!"

"I—I guess I got caught up in the moment," she explains lamely.

"You guys only did it once?"

"Well, no—"

"But you've never taken a peek, at all?"

"Christ, what are you? The sex police?"

"From the Alien Intercourse Investigation Unit," I deadpan.

"Ugh—"

"Because in the criminal justice system, alien encounters are considered to be especially heinous—"

She covers her face and lets out a long-suffering sigh.

"Okay," I tell her, "Here's what you're going to do. You go make up with Seven, then investigate and get back to me. I expect a full report."

She uncovers her face and asks, "Why don't you conduct your own alien peen investigation?"

"I don't have one to investigate."

She unclasps a clip from her hair then turns and throws it toward the wall. Before it can hit though, it's stopped in mid-air and seems to float.

Lu slowly un-camouflages, holding Mandy's clip in one tentacle.

"Oh, look who's here," she says nonchalantly.

She saunters over, retrieves her clip, and then she's leaving the room.

"I expect a full report," she calls over her shoulder.

CHAPTER TWENTY

—LU—

I breathe deeply and revel in Gloria's scent. She is pleased, happy to see me even though I was following her again. She told me that she is not terrified of me, that she does not find me offensive, and after our interlude in the pod access room, I have no option but to believe her.

"Well?" she asks.

"What?"

"Are you just going to stand there? Or are you going to disappear again as soon as I turn my back?"

I hold my hands up in supplication. "What would you like me to do?"

"C'mere so I can ask you some questions about this." She gestures toward a rendering of Homeworlder anatomy that has been projected onto the medbay wall.

Moving slowly so as not to startle her, I settle next to her and say, "Ask your questions."

"Are you sure? They're kind of intrusive questions now that I think about it."

"I will gladly help you understand anything you would like to know. I am honored by your interest in my species."

"Are you now?"

She has turned a little toward me and smiles.

This seems to be one of those rhetorical questions that humans do not require an answer to, but just in case I perform a human nod of ascent.

Her eyes sparkle and she is just so pretty. She smells good. Curious, happy, mischievous, and excited. And she has that underlying scent common to all females, but better.

She turns back to the anatomical map and gestures toward the center. "This is the area I'm curious about."

"That is the torsion plate mantle. It houses not only the torsion plates, but also the lower spinal cervix and coaxial—"

"Okay," She waves a hand dismissively. "That's all very interesting. But there are a couple of specific things I want to know about."

She glances down and my eyes follow to see that one of my tentacles has wound its way around her ankle and calf. She does not mind. She continues to smile at me, and her scent does not change. Well, it changes a little. She likes my touch. I do not understand it. The whole universe finds Homeworlders to be disgusting and offensive, but this human—

"I read up on octopuses just a little while ago and they have a thing called a syphon. They use it to swim by pushing water through it and it is where their waste is excreted from." She waves at the middle part of the projection. "I don't see a syphon anywhere."

That is an intrusive question.

I point to the crease labeled funnel between two tentacles on the side of the projected Homeworlder. "Here. It balloons while swimming but is discreet when dry."

"Ahh," she says in understanding. She nudges me with her elbow and says, "You're being a good sport about this. I appreciate it. I'll tell you what, when we're done answering my questions about Homeworlder anatomy, I can help you understand human anatomy. If you have any questions."

I perform a human nod. This is kind of her. I do have a few questions about humans.

She points at the projection again and asks, "So this is a penis?"

"That is an implantation arm."

"A what now?"

"An implantation arm. It is a sex organ."

"Okay, but what does it implant?" she asks, wide-eyed, "And why is it called an arm?"

"Homeworlders have only one sex. Where humans have a breeder type whose eggs are fertilized by an insemination type, Homeworlders have only one sex and it is the implantation type. When breeding a host, this sex organ implants eggs that use ambient DNA to self-fertilize." I point to the projection's two upper arms. "These are upper arms." I gesture to the bottom half. "These are tentacle arms." Then I point to the organ in question. "That is an implantation arm. This is how Homeworlders designate our limbs."

"Oh." She squeaks, then clears her throat and speaks in her regular voice, "I see."

A quiet fills the space between us and her scent is slightly tinged with alarm. I do not understand why she would find Homeworlder anatomy alarming. It is nothing to do with her.

"So, how many kids do Mandy and Seven have now? If every time they have sex—"

"Homeworlders are capable of pleasure-mating. Not every encounter is procreative."

"Okay, then why did he implant her at all?"

So that is the reason for her alarm. She is concerned for her fellow human.

"It happened once due to miscommunication."

"Huh?"

"There is a word in Earth-Human speak that means many different things and is often used as an expletive. Earth-Human speak was new to the translation matrix, and not all of the translations were being provided. Seven thought she was demanding that he breed her, demanding it very forcefully. She was only voicing her pleasure though. That was the miscommunication. If you would watch the sec—"

"I'm not watching the security footage of them fucking, Lu. That is just cringe. Quit suggesting it."

"As you say," I agree. "That is the word though, the one you just used for copulation. It has so many meanings it will not translate properly."

Another silence stretches between us. At least she is not alarmed anymore. I wonder if she is still willing to help me understand human anatomy. I get the basics. Humans are not so different from many other species. But the medbay AI has not cataloged human anatomy yet so there are some particulars that I wonder about.

"I guess it's kind of funny." She grins at me. "Mandy says something like 'fuck me' and Seven hears 'Put an egg in me right now!' I mean, I wouldn't want to be in that situation, but it's funny."

Talking with her so intimately about Homeworlder anatomy has fostered a closeness between us and I feel warm all over hearing her say those words, even in jest. She cannot know how shocking, how taboo it is. I know she is not saying these things to me, not really. But my body reacts nevertheless. And who could have guessed that any being in this galaxy would wish to speak of such things with me? As though my form is interesting and worthy of notice.

Her attention is heady, and it is having an undeniable effect and I am trying so hard to conceal it and pretend nonchalance that will allow this conversation to continue.

I have lost control of my coloring though, and it is spiraling in a riot of pinks and purples.

"So, your turn. What do you want to know about humans? You've been so patient with my intrusive questions, the least I can do is return the favor," she says.

It occurs to me that I should stop while she thinks well of me. What if I ask something that she takes offense to? Or something that alarms her?

"I have reconsidered. I do not want to ask you anything."

"Aw, c'mon, don't be like that. Here I am making a fool of myself with my rudeness and my nosiness and you're not going to ask anything? Just leave me feeling like an awkward jerk?"

I do not understand half of this, but it is clear that she very much wants me to ask something.

"Why do humans cover themselves so? Even when they are over-warm they remain covered." I pluck at the edge of her skirt with the tip of one tentacle.

"Well, it's kind of complicated. There are different religious edicts and social norms that require modesty. It is considered rude to show private parts of your body in public places. Also, there are very strict beauty standards. Many people wouldn't want to show off parts of their body that don't conform to those ideals. And the wrong sort of men see women who wear skimpy clothes as a come-on."

Something about this explanation has made her sad.

"That is complicated," I concede. "But on this ship you do not need to worry about it. You are not on Earth anymore, not be-holden to those edicts, norms, and ideals."

She laughs as though I have made a joke. "Yeah, I'll just keep my clothes on, though, thanks anyway."

"It does create an air of mystery," I tell her. "Like there is something secret and valuable being kept hidden when it is only a body."

She nods. "I can see that."

"And it makes one wonder exactly what humans look like."

She tilts her head, confused. "But you've seen naked humans. On the Seereechee ship."

"I did not look. I knew that they were unwillingly exposed and would not want to be seen that way. I made sure to focus on their faces. And I was very distracted with keeping you safe. I did not stop to study your form."

"Ah, Lu, you're such a sweetheart."

The meaning is unclear, but she smells pleased and she looks happy. I feel like I have done something right.

"So, you're curious about what humans look like without their clothes?"

"I am not asking you to—"

"But you're curious."

"Yes."

"Any area specifically that you're curious about?" She holds her arms out and poses as if I should point to a particular spot.

I do not point, but I look at her torso, where she is covered from her collarbone down to her upper thighs by two different garments and probably more garments underneath. I will not say it, but I would also like to know what she smells like without clothing to muffle the scent. I bet it is delicious—

"It's not really what I signed up for, but—" She pulls herself up onto the exam table she has been leaning against. "Okay, I'll play along."

My tentacles have not released from her lower legs. They continue their hold, wound around her following up onto the table. I turn toward her fully, eager to see anything she would like to show me.

"First though, some ground rules. One—" she waves a single digit at me, "you can look, but don't touch." We glance down to where I'm already touching her. "You can touch my legs, but not —not anywhere I'm about to show you."

I do a human nod and say, "Agreed."

"Secondly, I know you have an implant that records every-thing you see. I also know that you can delete those recordings."

"I will delete them," I assure her.

"I want the security feed shut off in this room until we leave."

Accessing ship security through my implant, I suspend sur-veillance of the medbay for the rest of the day.

"Done."

She grabs the bottom of her upper garment and pulls it over her head. She is wearing a smaller, tighter covering underneath and she pulls that off as well.

"These are breasts." She cups them in her hands as though presenting them to me. "They are for—"

"No need. I understand that mammals nurture their young with—"

"But that's not all they're for," she interjects. "They're also an erogenous zone for most humans." Her nimble little fingers pinch and pull on the tips. "They can be very sensitive. And touching them can be very stimulating."

"I see."

Her scent has changed dramatically. This excites her a lot, showing me her body, stimulating herself so I can see.

This is a very thorough demonstration.

She removes a tablet from the folds of her lower garment, then unwinds the whole thing from around her hips, placing it beside her in a heap when she is done. There is yet another garment underneath that she hooks with her thumbs and pulls down her legs and fully off her body.

Now she is naked. Fully bared in front of me. I just—I want to touch every part of her, saturate myself in her scent. If I thought my body was reacting to her before, it is nothing compared to now. My implantation arm, something I barely ever take notice of, is heavy and demanding, seeming to have come to life on its own.

I am glad she is up on that table, and my lower body is hidden from her view. Hopefully, I get myself under control before she notices.

"This is a *puh-see*," she explains with import, gesturing toward the apex of her thighs, directly under her navel. Even without clothes, this area is hidden by a small thatch of fur.

"That is not translating."

She huffs.

"Okay, well." She grasps one knee, bending it and angling up and to the side to fully expose a most private, delicate part of her. She touches an outermost fold. "This is the labia majora," she touches an inner fold, "this is the labia minora. Here is the vagina, urethra, and *cleh-tor-hiss*."

"That does not translate." My voice sounds odd to my own ears. Strained. I want so badly to touch her, to fully explore everything she is displaying to me. That would violate her rules though. She was very clear that I should not touch this—what she is showing me. This is difficult.

"The *cliht* is a very important part of a human female." She dips her fingers over her whole *puhs-eee*, and I can see they are now slick with moisture that she is rubbing onto her—"It is a very sensitive, very pleasurable part of our sexual anatomy."

I hear a loud rumbling purr, then realize it is me. I am making that sound. I take a deep breath, attempting to calm myself and control my reactions, but I only succeed in taking in more of her delicious scent and I cannot—

"Lu."

I look up at her face and she is flushed, her eyes hooded, pupils dilated. These are all signals. Her scent, her voice, her body are all telling me something—

"Lu, please."

"Y-yes? What do you need?" I can barely form words. I cannot function when she—

"Touch me—"

I do not hesitate. Reaching for her with hands and claws and tentacles I embrace her before she is done speaking. The rule does not matter when she obviously needs me.

I rub my cheek against hers, trilling and purring. My claws are grabbing and gently squeezing her soft form wherever I can reach, and I use the tip of a tentacle to soothe and stimulate her slick, delicious sex. The sensitive cups bumping and rubbing against all of those parts she has shown me, especially the oh-so-important *cleh-tor-hiss*.

She is keening, wiggling, and breathlessly demanding more. Securing her arms and legs with my much stronger tentacles, I pin her to the table. I hold her open to me so I can give her more of the stimulation she's begging for. And no matter how much I give her, she still wants more until she is demanding, "Fuck me, please, Lu, I need it—"

Even as I am shocked by her demand, my body complies, and my implantation arm spears into her of its own accord.

She squeals and tries to wiggle, but I'm holding her firmly as I fuck into the clasp of her body. The hot, slick, pulsing clutch of her is more than I can bear.

I cannot form words, just sounds. Purring, growling, and

trilling against her ear as I withdraw from her only to spear her again, harder, faster, more—

Desperately striving toward some all-important, unknown goal. I am distracted when she turns her face from mine and licks the tentacle that has been holding her arm down. It's too much, especially when her slick, pink tongue runs over the edge of a cup delivering an unexpected shock that tips me right over the edge.

I am dying. That is the only way to describe it. This human has killed me with pleasure and my whole body tenses as I die with one explosive pulse after another.

I am only peripherally aware of her yanking her limb free of the tentacle she had licked. Then she is wrapping her delicate arm around my back to hold me tight as she undulates under me once, twice, then tensing as she hisses through her teeth. Her whole body does a little shake and the part of her sheathing me is pulsing in a strangling grip, adding even more pleasure on top of too much. I feel her flimsy claws score my back.

"Lu."

It is too much to expect me to talk right now. I cannot form words. I purr for her though.

"You're kinda squishing me, big guy."

Oh.

Moving into a standing position, I pull her with me to the edge of the table so as not to break our connection.

This is better. Spread out before me, I can take in her tangled mane, flushed face, lax limbs. I see rows of circular marks where I had gripped her with my tentacle cups and a lazy, satisfied smile plays across her plush, human lips.

I study her teats. Breasts, as she called them. It seems a primitive, animalistic label for them. But that is appropriate at this moment as she is being mated, driven by base desires, seeking only pleasure and satisfaction.

They are sensitive, that is what she said. I wrap a tentacle around each, encircling, reshaping, and squeezing. It is only when I touch the very tips of her lovely breasts that she shows a response. Moaning and undulating against me is more encouragement than I need. I snake a tentacle around her waist to help me hold her still along with the two still holding her legs open where we are joined. Then I attach two tentacle cups to those delicate peaks, to pull and pinch and, oh, she really likes that. Her scent and her body where she squeezes down on me tell me that much.

I tighten my grip around her waist and pull her away and off of me, not all the way, but only enough to grant me space the yank her back.

The way her teats bounce, and jiggle is such an enticing display that I repeat the maneuver. Again and again, I move her back and forth along my implantation arm. It feels selfish, as though I am using her as a sleeve for my pleasure, but she is loving it. All it takes is a brief stroke of her *cliht* and she is keening then gasping and pulsing around me again.

"This is what you like?" I ask as I continue working her. She does not answer, only gasps. "This is why you seek me out? You flirt and show me your body? Because you want this from me?"

"Yes!" She gasps and then she is tensing, she is climaxing again. Pulsing and quivering even tighter than before. Another wave of pheromones overwhelms me, and it is all I can stand. I cannot take any more. When I climax this time it is even more soul-shattering than the last, as though my very being has fragmented into shards of pleasure.

As I return to myself, I am shocked by what has happened. I am fundamentally changed, and I cannot go back to the being I was before I encountered this human. I hope she realizes that we are now linked. Our fates, our feelings, our lives, our bodies, everything. We belong together. I am sure she feels the same.

CHAPTER TWENTY-ONE
—GLORIA—

The space station is not what I thought it would be. I was expecting some sci-fi, space-age, star-trek-looking stuff. All shiny chrome and sparkly clean. But it's more like a mall. Shops, shops, and more shops. And plants. Towering trees, creeping vines, moss, ferns. There is a plant in every available space.

When we were approaching the space station earlier, we got a look at it. Not through a window or anything. Apparently, windows in space aren't a thing because they compromise the structural integrity of the wall/hull/whatever. Ken projected an image of it on the wall of a security alcove for us. From the outside, it looks pretty cool. There is this big metal rod and then these hula-hoop-looking things that spin around it. There are about a dozen hula hoops and the spinning is what creates their artificial gravity. Hoops aren't connected to each other in any way. If you need to access more than one, you've got to get back on your shuttle and dock at the next one.

Anyway, I was really impressed. It looked super-cool. But then when we got inside it was kind of a letdown. None of these shops are like stores on Earth. Like, there's usually a counter in front and a sign, and the shopkeeper gets whatever it is you want from the back and brings it out to you. It sucks. How do I know if I want something if I don't see it first?

I feel let down. But we aren't actually here to shop anyway. We're here about our membership with the Trader's Guild.

Mandy and Seven thought it was a given, but apparently not. We were surprised that our membership wasn't immediately approved because the Trader's Guild is known for taking anybody. Slavers, war criminals, it doesn't matter.

They draw the line at humans because they think we're animals. You know how parrots can talk and some chimps can do sign language and dogs can understand all sorts of commands? These Trader's Guild big-wigs think that about humans.

All of Mandy's money-making schemes are put on hold for now because every single one hinges on Trader's Guild membership. She's been talking about starting her own guild if this doesn't work out, but that would be a hassle. That would take time and energy away from tracking down and rescuing all the abducted humans which is her ultimate goal.

Anyway, it's Ken, Mandy, and I on the space station. We've left Lu and Seven on the ship. Seven is staying with the babies because one of them keeps escaping. They are supposed to stay in that tank for months, almost a year, to develop their lungs. But one of them must be very precocious because it keeps leaping out of the tank and trying to leave the room. I've met the kids and Mandy has shown me all kinds of videos. They mostly look like Homeworlders with a couple of human features thrown in here and there. And they're Barbie-doll sized. One out of the four looks very human though, with legs instead of tentacles. They're the one that keeps escaping. They can't swim as well as the others, so they have a series of platforms that they hang out on when they need a break. They've been using those platforms to leap out of the tank though. And one time they made it all the way out into the hallway where Peach started chasing them. It was awful.

So, anyway, Seven has to stay with the kids. And Lu is keeping an eye on the ship.

When we showed up at the Guild Office though, I wasn't on the list for the appointment, only Mandy and Ken. Now I'm moping around this boring-ass space station while I wait for them.

My mind keeps wandering back to Lu. Less than three hours

ago, I fucked an alien. Not just that. I seduced him, stripped naked, showed him the goods, and begged him to touch me.

What is wrong with me?

I think it's something about Lu personally that makes me act this way. It has occurred to me that I might just have an alien kink or a tentacle fetish. But I don't feel drawn to Ken or Seven the way I do to Lu. It's personal. But does it mean anything? And are there going to be any consequences for my actions?

I just don't know. I shake these thoughts off and try to focus on my surroundings.

There are so many different kinds of aliens. Most of them look like animal/human hybrids. Like, dog people, cat people, lizard people, bird people, etc. Apparently, all of these aliens share a genetic heritage with humans. There are a couple that obviously don't though. There is a being that looks like a column of floating chalk dust. I almost bumped into them, but when I got close I felt icy-cold. I changed direction and that's when I noticed other aliens nodding and talking with the dust column. There's another alien that looks like a balloon cinched with belts. I guess the air inside is the alien being. Besides those two very alien aliens, all of the rest are obviously related to humans and other Earth creatures.

I can't read the signs on any of these shops. There are pictures of things like machines, clothes, food, but I just don't feel confident enough to walk up to a counter and ask an alien about their wares, until I get to the Earth Human Shop.

Unlike the others, this tiny shop has an open layout. There are three counters with human stuff displayed on them. Books, clothes, toiletries. Some of them are obvious forgeries. Like some of the books don't open, no pages, just a block painted like a book. And there's a hairbrush with no bristles, just bumps. Useless.

When I walked into the shop, I heard a recording telling me that this was the finest shop with the largest collection of Earth-Human accessories. I'm confused because, from what Mandy said, I thought all of the humans were dispersed and enslaved.

How is there a market for human accessories? Especially these ones that make no sense.

I'm walking along trying to figure this place out when I see a Mortal Kombat vs DC Universe disc for PlayStation 3. It's a scratched-up disc without a case, but oh my gosh, it almost makes me cry. I miss gaming so much. Of course, these aliens don't understand, and Mandy isn't any kind of a gamer. I've tucked this feeling away and tried to find new hobbies. But Mortal Kombat! I gingerly pick up the disc like it's something rare and precious. I want it. I don't pay attention to what I'm doing, but I'm cradling it against my chest as I try and figure out how to buy it. I realize I don't have any credits. I'm going to have to leave it here and come back for it when Mandy and Ken are done with their appointment.

I hear a hiss and a growl behind me that translates to, "Please do not handle the merchandise."

I look and it's one of the lizard-aliens. About seven and a half feet tall with teal scales, a long thick tail, and a muzzle that comes about a foot out of his face, and a mouth full of sharp pointy teeth.

"By the Chaos That Consumes all Things!" he exclaims when he sees me.

It takes me a moment to realize it's an expletive, like "oh, my God" or "what the hell."

Cleary, he's surprised to see a human in his human shop.

I gather my courage and say, "Hi, do you have any more of these?" I hold up the disc. "Or maybe a console to go with it?"

He opens his muzzle to speak, then closes it. Opens it again and says, "Yes, I have more of those and a console in the back."

My heart soars. I might be able to actually play Mortal Kombat!

He's walking toward the door at the back of the shop. I follow him.

"Do you have a TV to hook it up to? Controllers?"

He bobs his head. "Yes, all of those things. In perfect condition."

Oh, wow!

"So they work? Do you have a converter or something to plug them in?"

"Of course."

He opens the door and motions that I should go through ahead of him. When I do, I feel a claw comb through my hair next to my ear, snagging on my translation clip and yanking it off.

I whirl around and yell, "Hey—"

But it's too late, he's closed the door.

I stand there in the dark, mouth agape. I'm such a fucking idiot! How could I have just—

I hear a snick sound and from one moment to the next there's no air. I can't breathe. I gape and gasp like a fish out of water, but nothing. I'm dying. For a fucking Mortal Kombat game! I fall over onto the floor, lungs burning, eyes watering.

How long does it take to suffocate? This is absolute burning agony.

I pass out.

CHAPTER TWENTY-TWO

—LU—

Tiny is sobbing. I have never seen a human so distraught. It is truly terrible. She is leaking out of her eyes and nose. She is trying to speak, but she keeps gasping, wailing, and sniffling so we cannot understand her. After giving her a few moments to make herself understood, I turn to Ken.

"What is the issue with this human?"

"She is distraught."

I wait for further explanation, but then I notice that it is only the two of them.

"Where is Gloria?"

"She's gone!" Tiny wails.

"Gone?"

Seven has barged into the shuttle bay and scoops Tiny up into his arms, petting her and trilling to calm her down.

My implant starts working overtime as Ken transfers security logs from the space station so I can see for myself what has happened.

Gloria went into a store and never came out. A few moments after she went in, the storefront closed, the security door shut, and the projected sign dimmed. I rewind a bit to read the sign:

Risant's Best Human Supplies and Accessories
Only the Best for Your Human

This does not make any sense. Everybody knows that humans are a sentient people. Why would there be such a store that seems to cater to owners of human pets?

And what is this proprietor doing with Gloria? Does he think that she is some sort of stray animal that wandered into his shop?

"Lu."

I try to focus on the store. Perhaps I can hear what is said. But it is useless. Accessing the other files Ken sent me I find a still photo of the shop owner. I have never seen this person before. He is the same lizard-like species as our trade partner, Salhuteck, but that does not really signify anything.

"Lu."

The shop owner's name is Far'Shep. I do not recognize it at all.

Security logs show that soon after closing his shop, he transported a hover cart to a space shuttle, docked with an orbiting ship, then folded space, leaving this sector.

I have no way to track him. Gloria is lost. Anything could be happening to her. As I stand here useless, she could be hurt or scared. She is probably praying I come rescue her, but how can I —?

"Lu." It is Ken trying to speak with me.

"What?"

"I have contracted with Shafeenah. She is on her way."

I do not know that name. "Who is she?"

"A bounty hunter associated with the Trader's Guild. Tiny has contracted with her previously."

Good. That is the logical thing to do. But—

"Do you think..." I try to form my worry into words. "Are we sure she was taken against her will?"

He is stupefied by this question, tentacles all scrunched, colors darkly swirling.

"Yes! Of course, she was taken! Lu, she is enamored with you. And she is a good friend to Mandy. And she left her animal!" He holds up the furry little beast in question. With a tentacle securely wrapped around the animal's middle, he waves the panting thing back and forth. "She would not leave Princess Peach!"

I nod. He is correct. She would never leave Princess Peach.

"Tiny is an emotional mess," Ken tells me. "She is distraught because she blames herself. It is making her useless."

I nod in understanding.

"Seven is useless to us as well because he is focused solely on Tiny and his spawn. He does not seem to care about anybody else's well-being."

I nod again. That is understandable.

"It is up to us. We need to focus on finding Gloria! Quickly! We need to figure out why this shopkeeper took her. Where did he take her? How can we get her back?"

This is true. He is exactly right.

"Let us waste no time. We must direct our mental energy where it is useful!"

"Of course."

A few minutes later, there is a ping to notify us that a shuttle has docked.

"That will be Shafeenah." Ken turns toward the port opening in the shuttle bay and greats our guest.

She is a Felistae. As a people, they tend to be covered in shimmery blue fur. The males of her kind have great bushy manes around their faces. Being a female, she only has short, sleek fur leaving the large ears on top her head exposed. They move about as she listens.

This was very quick. Ken must have contacted her before he left the station.

Our bounty hunter wastes no time. She gets straight to the point and informs us, "I have issued a bounty on your human for twice the credits a human goes for in the slave market. I hope you have the funds to cover this."

"Yes."

"We do." Ken and I speak at the same time.

"Good." She looks from one to the other of us then says, "I will start by questioning the neighboring shopkeepers. Then I will follow up on leads. Then I will look for her at Seereechee trade grounds."

This sounds—good.

"I need backup. My partner is otherwise engaged. Will either one of you be able to serve in this capacity?"

I quickly hold up three tentacles and say, "I will be back up."

She gives me a toothy grin. "Good. Perfect." She looks around and then back at me. "Where is your creepy associate?"

Ken and I look at each other, equally confused, then back at her.

"The Arana-Vora?" she prompts.

"Oh, you mean Baht," Ken replies. "He is not here. Has not been with us since we got Lu back from the Seereechees."

She dips her chin and then holds up a furry hand to beckon me. "Alright then, friend, let us go question some shop keepers. No time like the present!"

I follow her into her shuttle feeling optimistic. Shafeenah is clearly a professional who knows what she's doing. I hope we can get Gloria back before the end of the day.

Before I close the port, I turn to Ken. "Thank you."

"Of course." He taps a closed fist against his heart to signify our solidarity in this matter, then assures me, "We will find her. I am certain of it."

CHAPTER TWENTY-THREE

—GLORIA—

I wake up and that's the good news. I'm alive.

The bad news is that I'm in a cage. Again! It's like a giant dog crate, with bars on the sides and front. It keeps being lifted, moved, and set back down.

My alien captor keeps giving me cookies that I immediately throw back out at him. He'll laugh, make alien noises at me that I can't understand because he stole my translator, and then he wags a finger at me.

This fucking bastard is so pleased with himself.

There's another alien here somewhere. I keep hearing them speak, but I haven't seen them yet. They're probably the same species because they hiss and growl in the same language.

I know that he can understand me because he still has his implant, even if I don't have my translator. Instead of answering me when I ask why he's kidnapped me and where he's taking me, he just tries to give me more cookies and makes noises at me.

When I flip him off and tell him to go fuck himself, he laughs at me some more.

Eventually, I'm loaded onto a shuttle and flown down to a planet's surface. It is a desert. Sand and rocks as far as I can see in one direction. There is a little town with roads and buildings and houses in the other direction.

My cage is on a hover-cart that follows my kidnapper down a narrow road and up to a house.

The houses are all the same color as the sand which is a dark tan. They're boring, like tan boxes with little windows and doors.

He must be expected because when he stands in front of a door, it just opens and the lizard-alien who opens it is delighted, just ecstatic to see us. They clap their hands and make excited noises and call over their shoulder. Two more lizard-aliens come to the door and are equally happy to see us.

There is some discussion and eventually the alien that brought me here leaves.

This is bad news. I mean, I hate the kidnapping bastard, but every time I'm moved or change hands, I'm that much further away from being rescued. Fortunately, I'm one hundred percent sure I'm eventually going to be rescued. Because Lu is obsessed with me and totally in love with me. He's not going to let me stay kidnapped. I know this for an absolute fact.

Thinking about Lu makes me feel kind of down though because right after we had sex, I blew him off. We cuddled on the medbay table for a moment, but then I got up and went to the bathroom. Went for a snack and back to my room to nap until we got to the station. I'm conflicted about the whole alien-sex thing. I needed that snack and a nap. It's hard to admit to myself, but it was the best, hottest sex I ever had. What does that mean? Why would I enjoy it more with a tentacled alien guy than a regular human guy?

I needed space, just to think it over.

I'm such an asshole. I'm pretty sure that was his first time and it's so obvious how he feels about me and me just—

Anyway, whenever he rescues me, I'm going to fix it. I'm going to be so sweet to him. He's going to be the happiest freaking alien in the whole universe, I'll make sure of it.

But then an awful thought occurs to me. What if Lu thinks I left on purpose? What if Mandy and everyone else think that, too, and they don't come looking for me? What will happen here with these lizard-aliens?

No, they have to know better.

Instead of going into the house I've just been delivered to, the two lizard-aliens, who are both a dull red, close the door and start making their way down the street with the hover-cart my dog-crate is on following them.

We pass by a few other lizard-aliens, and I try to yell for help, but they either don't understand me or don't care. We get to a giant house. Where all the other houses look like sandstone cubes, this one looks like at least twenty of those all stuck together.

My captors stand quietly in front of this door for a good thirty seconds before it opens and the lizard guy that opens it is not happy. In fact, he looks kind of serious? Formal? I decide that he's a butler.

"Help!" I yell at him, grabbing the bars of my cage. "I've been kidnapped! Help me!"

He just moves to the side and motions that I and my kidnappers should come in. We move through several rooms until my cage is set up in a corner.

Then the two red lizard guys leave.

The butler leaves.

This is bad. I've been moved to three different locations and changed hands twice. Lu, Mandy, and Ken might not be able to find me. If I ever get back, I'm going to ask for some kind of tracking chip or shot or something. Then even if my translator is gone, I could still be found. I mean, I've had some bad luck with abductions lately. First those men at the beach house, then those gray aliens, then those government people, and now these lizard-aliens. I need a tracking implant.

I hear footsteps padding toward me and I look up expecting the lizard-alien butler or another one like him, but it's not.

It's a human. A naked human man. A really good-looking one.

I'm so shocked that I don't even say anything. He doesn't notice me at first and I have time to study him. He is muscular, like an underwear-model level of fit. He has medium brown skin and short black hair that is tightly curled. His skin is perfect, like all of it, and I can see all of it, it's flawless and shiny with some kind of oil. His hair, too. He has sharp cheekbones and a strong jawline, generous lips, and a slightly wide nose. Very strong, handsome features. This might be the most attractive guy I have ever seen in person. When he finally looks up from the tablet he's carrying and notices me, I see that his eyes are a warm, light brown and his lashes are so long. How come men always have the longest, thickest eyelashes? That's just not fair.

He holds his tablet closer to his face and says, "Call Sal."

I hear a hissing growl come from the tablet, then Human Guy says, "Sal, there's a human woman in a cage in the study."

Even his voice is attractive, one of those very deep, rich masculine voices.

More hissing and growling from the tablet.

"Okay. I'll stay with her."

He comes closer to my cage and peers inside. I notice that he's wearing a band of silver mesh around his neck with a D-shaped ring attached. Like a dog collar. He asks, "Are you alright?"

"No! I've been kidnapped!" I tell him. "Please get me out."

He runs his hands all over the cage trying to figure out how to open it, but he finally gives up and says, "Sal will open it. He should be here soon."

"Is Sal one of the lizard-aliens?"

He nods.

"I don't—"

I shut up because just then a very fancy lizard-alien walks in. He's leaf-green and all of his scales shine. He has jewelry, armbands, belts, bracelets, necklaces, and rings. All swirling designs of shiny silver. He even has a few silver bands encircling his tail.

The guy steps away from my cage to talk to him.

He growls and hisses at the human as he pets his head and combs his claws through his tightly curled hair.

The guy seems to lean into it.

I'm starting to get a bad feeling.

The guy says, "Well, she needs a translation cuff, and she

wants out of this cage."

More growling and hissing.

"Okay, well, go get it. I'll stay with her."

The lizard looks slightly affronted but turns and leaves the room anyway.

"So, bad news first." the guy says.

"Okay."

"You're going to have to take those clothes off. It's considered extremely insulting to cover up your body on this planet."

"Well, I consider it extremely insulting to kidnap me, steal my translator, and lock me in a cage!"

He laughs showing off straight white teeth. I don't know what he thinks is so funny.

"The good news," he says. "Is that Sal bought you as a gift. For me."

He comes right up to my cage and peers inside at me. "Don't worry. I'm going to be real nice to you."

CHAPTER TWENTY-FOUR

—GLORIA—

These Lizard fuck-faces are officially my least favorite species in the whole universe.

I know it's not right to make sweeping generalizations about a whole species of people after interacting with only a few of them, but it's obvious to me that this whole planet must condone slavery. Not just enslaving humans, other species are living in bondage here. The worst example I've seen is tiny little fairy people that are kept in an over large birdcage. I've tried to talk with them. I can understand them with the translator, but they are listless, barely ever speaking, and when they do it's a single word at a time that doesn't seem to apply to anything. Like, "Drinks." Another will say, "Dew." And another will say, "Evenings." Then they're quiet for the rest of the day.

Poor things.

And the lizards act like I'm a rude guest. Like I chose to come here and should appreciate their hospitality. Ugh. I hate them.

Shawn, the human guy, is almost as bad. Just like he'd predicted, my clothes had been taken away. When I asked for them back, everybody acted like I was being unbearably rude. I was always the rude one, the bad one, making situations awkward, making lizards uncomfortable. Shawn is the good, well-behaved human.

I'm so frickin tired of it.

Shawn goes on and on about wanting to go back to Earth.

When I told him that if he'd just help me, Mandy will take him right back to Earth whenever he wanted, it was a no-go. He doesn't trust Homeworlders, and he thinks Mandy and I have been brainwashed or have Stockholm syndrome or something.

How he trusts these kidnapping, enslaving, lizard fucks, but not me or Mandy or the people we vouch for, I just don't know.

I think he likes it here. He likes the boss lizard guy who is always petting his hair and talking sweetly to him with endearments and cute nicknames.

Sal, the fancy lizard boss, says that he's working on getting Shawn back to Earth, but Mandy won't allow Sal to take him. I have a few guesses as to why that is. If she is trying to protect Earth from slavers, these lizards are the last sort who should be granted any kind of access.

Finally, I just had to ask over breakfast one morning, "Shawn, you seem to like your life here with Sal. Why do you even want to get back to Earth?"

"What do you mean? I'm a human. I belong with other humans. You don't want to go back?"

"Nope. Never."

"Why not?"

"I've already been back once, and I was detained in some sort of secret government facility. I wasn't treated well."

"For real? I hadn't considered that. You don't think there's a way around it?"

"Nope. If you go back, they'll track you down before you even land, point a gun at you then escort you to a facility. They said that I wasn't under arrest, that it was quarantine. Same difference here, though, I'm being detained indefinitely without any way to communicate with the outside world."

He sips his drink thoughtfully, but he doesn't seem too upset by the prospect.

One thing I can't fault Sal for is his food. All of the meals are delicious. Well-seasoned meat dishes, fruits, veggies, all good stuff.

I was surprised to learn that Shawn and Mandy have a history. They were abducted at the same time. But there's some kind of beef between them. Shawn won't explain any of it.

Anyway, this whole situation is fucked up. Every lizard in this house keeps telling Shawn that I need discipline and correction, but Shawn keeps copping an attitude and bragging that I'm his human, gifted to him by Salhuteck and nobody gets to touch me or correct me without his say so. One time, I insulted one of Sal's guests, just in my usual way of calling all of these lizards names and cussing them out. But I guess this guest was more important than anybody else I had insulted. They demanded that there should be some kind of consequence for the insult, and Shawn ended up being punished for it.

He won't talk about what sort of punishment it was. With their medical technology, he could have been very badly hurt and I wouldn't know because they'd just heal him up before I saw him again.

It's a really awkward situation. Like, I instinctively feel grateful to Shawn for protecting me and sticking up for me. And even though his "I'm going to be so nice to you" declaration sounded like a sexual come-on, it wasn't. He is legit trying to be nice to me. But how grateful can I be to someone who owns me? Who won't let me get free and get back to my home and my friends? Back to Lu?

That's something I can't talk to Shawn about. He has a real prejudice against Homeworlders. When I talk about wanting to go home, I'll say I miss wearing clothes, I miss my dog, I miss Mandy. I can't say I miss Lu because that will just piss Shawn off.

I do miss Lu, though. That's the real reason why staying here isn't even an option. Ever since I first "discovered" him in that cove, I've felt like Lu belongs to me. And even though I didn't take the time to talk with him about it after we had sex, I felt like that intimacy cemented things between us. Like, we understood each other and knew that we both wanted to be together.

Anyway, all that's out the frickin window if I can't figure out how to escape this lizard planet.

"It doesn't sound like they really hurt you," Shawn says,

bringing my attention back to our conversation about my detention on Earth. "And when more humans come back, well they wouldn't bother detaining us all, would they?"

"Yes, they would," I argue, "And if it's too much hassle, they would just kill us. They aren't going to let people loose after being abducted by aliens."

"Hmm."

"It might not have physically hurt, but that was the worst time of my life. I've not had an easy life, but feeling so isolated, not having any options or distractions. It was hell. Psychological torture. I never want to go back. I wouldn't wish that experience on anyone."

He nods. I can tell that I've given him something to think about.

CHAPTER TWENTY-FIVE

—LU—

"She doesn't want to come back."

Tiny's words rip through me. I can tell that she is not lying, but it cannot be true. I will not believe it.

"I saw a video of her saying that she never wants to come back here. That we tortured her and—"

"That is not true! She was happy here—"

Tiny is shaking her head in negation. "I thought so, too, but maybe—I guess she felt trapped? And like she didn't have any options?"

This is not right. "Did you speak with her? Did she tell you these things herself?"

"No." Now Tiny is in real distress. Her eyes are leaking. "No, Sal said she didn't want to ever see any of us again."

"Sal is a lying, degenerate slaver! We can't trust anything he says!"

"But I saw the video. She said she hated it here!"

"Videos can be manipulated and he knows you do not have an implant to interface and check veracity. This is a trick! It must be—"

Tiny takes a deep breath and says, "I know that you two were close, but maybe she was just making the best of a bad situation? Choosing the lesser of two evils? And now that she has options, she just—well, she doesn't choose us."

"No!"

"But—"

"No! I will not believe this! Not unless I hear it directly from her." I realize that I am yelling at Tiny, and I quiet myself.

She is obviously upset, nearly as upset as I am.

How can she believe this though? That Gloria thinks badly of us. That Gloria does not wish to return to us? How can she take the word of Salhuteck?

"I need to go check on the babies," she says and quickly leaves the shuttle bay.

I had been so happy, so optimistic just a few hours ago. After a week-long investigation, Shafeenah was able to track down the operation that kidnapped Gloria. It is a human rescue operation. Those stores are meant to draw in owners of "human pets" and then track down those humans and rescue them. And here, Gloria had just blundered in. What they thought would take them months, tracking down a human and organizing their rescue/escape they were able to accomplish in moments when Gloria, a "stray" just wandered into their trap.

It was Salhuteck behind the whole thing. Trying to expand his human collection by rehoming abused and enslaved humans.

Like his planet is any better. Like he himself is not a slaver.

And I am supposed to believe that Gloria picks him over me?

I do not accept this.

She gave herself to me. We are meant to be together. This is obvious.

I am pacing back and forth across the shuttle bay as I try to think, to come up with a plan. I need to speak with Gloria and if she tells me that she does not want to be with me, then I will believe. If she wishes to live the life of a pampered slave on that desert world, it is her choice. But I need to hear it from her.

And what will I do if I do not like her answer? Can I really just let her go? I can at least make my case. Tell her everything, put all of my feelings and intentions into words so that she knows, without any doubt, that I am hers.

I hear a noise at the door and look up to see that Tiny has

returned and has Seven with her.

"Okay, Lu, I've talked about it with Seven and he agrees with you." She pats Seven's tentacle where he is holding her around her waist. "We can't trust Sal. So, we are going to sanction him until we get to speak to Gloria face to face."

"Sanction him?"

She nods. "Yes. We won't trade with him, and we won't do business with anybody who trades with him until he arranges a meeting between us and Gloria. You're right, we need to hear directly from her."

I nod. "Thank you. It is a good plan."

Salhuteck has made a fortune on Tiny's Earth-Human Art. He would not like to find himself cut out of any future deals.

"Do you have a new product or campaign? We can comm him to discuss it and then—"

"And then be like, but not until we speak with Gloria!" Tiny interrupts excitedly. "You're right! That's the quickest way to let him know what's going on."

"But who will we tell him we are doing business with instead?" Seven asks.

"We do not have to give him a name," I answer. "He has undoubtably heard of our recent application to the Trader's Guild. He knows we have options."

"Okay, alright, so we just need to go to the storage bay and find some human stuff that Sal would be excited to buy." Tiny is already headed down the corridor and I hurry to catch up.

When we get to the storage bay, we find Ken reorganizing it again. We then get into a rather tedious discussion over who owns the right to sell these Earth things. Ken has discovered a copyright symbol that is etched on most of them. Tiny maintains that she has the right to sell them "second hand" and Ken points out that she will need to disclose the fact that we cannot grant any kind of permissions where these products are concerned.

"Of course, Ken," Tiny agrees, clearly exasperated. "But only after we get Gloria back. I'm not going to disclose anything until our demands are met."

Ken nods, satisfied. Then he asks, "Did you all discuss the updates?"

Tiny looks from him to me, then Seven. "What updates?"

I access the ship logs through my implant as Ken explains, "We have leads on four humans. One may be crashed and stranded on an R-class planet. One was bought by a Royal House, and two more are being hosted under refugee status on a space station."

"Why do you insist on using that word?" Seven asks.

"Because that was the word they used in the report. Try to focus on something other than your deviancies."

Seven snarls. Ken growls. This is a silly argument. "Host" is a word like any other, with multiple meanings. It does have an offensive connotation in regard to us Homeworlders, but that does not mean that every utterance of it is offensive.

"We need to focus," Tiny interjects. "First priority," she holds up one digit, "is to speak with Gloria and bring her home if that's what she wants." She holds up another digit. "Secondly, we need to be firm with Salhuteck. He cannot continue his human rescue operation if he's going to keep rehoming humans. He can't just collect us like stray kittens." She holds up another digit. "And thirdly, we'll follow up on all of those leads while," she raises a fourth digit, "setting up a human camp on one of the uninhabited planets or moons in the Solar System. We can't just keep extra humans we don't know anything about on our ship. And we can't send them back to Earth in good conscience if we know they are going to be detained and mistreated."

Seven and Ken both *click* in agreement. I click as well after considering for a second.

I don't really care about anything else on that list besides retrieving Gloria.

CHAPTER TWENTY-SIX

—LU—

Tiny is frustrated with me for the whole shuttle ride down to Salhuteck's residence. She keeps insisting that she should go alone, but she has no good arguments for that. On Earth, it made sense because that is her home and her government. She would know best. But I've known Salhuteck longer than she has. I have many years of experience as a trader dealing with dishonest, unethical types. Tiny is just too pure for this business. Where does all of her blind trust and unwavering optimism spring from? Maybe it is a human trait, but you should not just operate under the assumption that people are telling you the truth. Especially not people like Salhuteck.

It only took Salhuteck an hour to agree to our demands. He could not conceal his greed and excitement as Tiny alluded to a whole shipment of earth products created by many different artisans. It was a sight when he completely lost composure at the news of the sanction.

Oh, he was furious.

"How can I trade with a being who kidnaps and holds humans hostage?" She shook her head in mock-dejection. "Sal, I have valued you as trade partner and I don't pretend to understand your culture. I just can't—" Then she made a sobbing noise and turned away from the com screen.

Then Seven took over negotiations, berating Sal for upsetting his mate, snarling, and growling, and then saying in no uncertain terms that we would not be trading with him until Tiny meets with Gloria in person and is assured of her well-being.

Sal blustered, complained, wheedled, and finally threatened. He would report us to the guild, the federation, and on and on.

Seven ended the comm.

Sal called back to arrange the meeting and end Tiny's sanctions before this "misunderstanding goes any further".

And Tiny thought she would go alone to this hostile negotiation with a slaver, a human-thief who had already tricked her once?

Seven, Ken, and I all felt that any one of us would be safer representing our cause than her.

Finally, we came to an agreement. Seven would stay with the babies. Ken would man the ship and I would accompany Tiny to meet with Gloria.

If it comes to violence and threats, I am experienced with such things now. I am willing to meet violence with violence if it gets Gloria safely home.

How is Tiny planning to accomplish this goal? Just flash her blunt human teeth and toss her mane around?

She grumbles and complains the whole shuttle ride.

Why she always wants to go it alone, I cannot say. It will not be allowed in this situation though.

We are greeted as honored guests when we arrive, then shown into a comfortable room and offered refreshments.

Tiny goes to actually drink what is offered to her and I have to snatch it out of her grasp.

"Do not trust these people," I warn her.

"Oh, right. You're right."

I set the drink on a nearby table.

Salhuteck enters the room. He is bedecked in silver jewelry that adorns every visible limb and his neck as well. His green scales are polished to a shine, and he holds his head high as if he is not the lowest sort of criminal.

Behind him is a naked human, his beloved Shawn, who he bought from Seereechees more than a year ago. He treats Shawn like a favored concubine more than a slave, pampering him and spoiling him. The male is an especially striking human. I can understand why Sal is enamored of him. Shawn has had many opportunities to leave Salhuteck's care, but he has never taken advantage of any.

Is it possible that Gloria is also happy in his care? I do not want to consider it, but—

She enters the room at Shawn's side, unabashedly naked, her arm entwined with his, holding on for dear life as though she would hate to be separated from him.

All of my tentacles still as my hearts stutter and a cold dread clenches inside of me.

This is the truth. It was not a trick. Gloria really does not want me. Why would she when she has this adorable human man and this opulent residence where she will be spoiled and catered to?

Of course, she would not pick me when she has a choice.

It is a stabbing, physical pain through my hearts and I just cannot— I do not need to be here for this. I should never have come.

Stupid, stupid, stupid! I berate myself as I instinctually camouflage and flee the room as soon as the path is clear.

This is why Tiny kept insisting she should come alone. She knew or at least suspected this outcome.

Perhaps Gloria did not see me? Hopefully, she does not realize what a desperate, lovesick idiot I am to have chased her all the way to this awful planet.

She really just left me. After being intimate with me, making me feel like— She found the first opportunity on that space station and left me. She has been living happily with this male the whole time.

How could I have been so mistaken?

How ridiculous to think of us as a couple? Me, so monstrous and alien to her and her this perfect, beautiful...

I presumed so much. Just assumed that she would feel with the same intensity when all it ever was...

I cannot get this void-sent door open! I have made it all the way to the main entrance of the house, but it is locked. Of all the blasted indignities.

"Hey!" I feel a sharp tug on one of my tentacles. I shake it off and try to open the door by force, shoving myself against it. I will not be kept here.

"Lu! Just what the hell do you think you're doing?"

It is her. In a final humiliation, she has chased me down before I could make an escape.

CHAPTER TWENTY-SEVEN

—GLORIA—

I have been through a rollercoaster of emotions today. First, I woke up late in a comfortable bed and ate a delicious breakfast. That was nice. Since then I have been harassed, manipulated, tricked, ignored and right now I'm as pissed off as I have ever been in my whole life.

So Lu was just going to leave me here? Really? He tried to camouflage and sneak out like I wouldn't even know he was there to start with!

I was so relieved when I saw it was him and Mandy in that room.

Sal had made such a big deal when he told Shawn, "A valued trade partner is interested in your human—"

"What?"

"No!"

Shawn and I both yelled at the same time.

"I am delighted that you are in agreement. I, too, wish for Gloria to stay with us and do not want to hand her over to these others."

I have a hard time reading these lizard-alien faces, but Sal looked sneaky. The way his skinny forked tongue kept popping out was weird. It seemed like a nervous tic or a tell. It seemed like he was lying about something. But what? What could be worse than some other aliens wanting to own me?

"Don't worry, we're not selling you," Shawn says.

I'm sure he means to be reassuring. But, with my luck, I'm being sold. They're going to offer too much money, or some bribe or threat and I'm going to be handed over to these new aliens. And then what will happen to me?

It's not like Shawn has any real power here. What are his promises worth in this situation?

I've lucked out so far. Even though I've been kidnapped and held against my will, I haven't been physically hurt. That could change. It for real could. These new aliens could have terrible plans for me.

Why have I been such a god-awful bitch to everyone on this planet? I should have been charming and agreeable and ingratiated myself so that Shawn and Sal would never, ever think to—

"Hey, I promise we're not letting anyone else get you."

Shawn carefully wraps an arm around me and I kind of freeze up. He hasn't touched me before, and I don't like it. I hope it doesn't signal some sort of change in our relationship. So far, he's been treating me with kid gloves, very careful of my boundaries and my feelings. I'm worried that him hugging me like this will lead to more, and I don't want that.

I take a deep breath and remind myself to be nice. Ingratiate myself to him. I hug him back. It is a weird, naked hug.

Not for the first time, I wonder what Shawn's deal is. Does he really think that he owns me? If he thinks that why hasn't he made any demands? What exactly is his relationship with these lizard-aliens?

So far, Sal seems to cater to Shawn and indulge him no matter what kind of attitude Shawn has about it. While Shawn passes that same treatment on to me. But Shawn wants me, he doesn't hide that. He can't hide a lot of his reactions when he's naked all the time and I can't blame him for looking and reacting when I'm also naked all the time. But never, not once, has he done a single thing to sexually proposition me.

I'm grateful, but also confused. And relieved. I don't want Shawn. He's really attractive, and if I had met him a year ago... maybe.

But I miss Lu. I miss him so much it's like grieving. I want him following me around everywhere. I want Lu comforting me, not this naked human guy.

I want to be passed on to some other alien even less, though.

Anyway, by the time this meeting happens, I'm all anxious and worked up. Shawn and Sal have both assured me multiple times that I'm staying with them no matter what. But they aren't exactly trustworthy, are they?

Sal explained that we had to meet with these aliens because they are very important trade partners that he doesn't want to offend. He's going to let them see me and hear them out.

As Sal goes through the door, I try to hang back. I hold on to Shawn's arm and quietly tell him, "Let's run! Let's just get out of here and comm Mandy, she'll come get us!"

Shawn just shakes his head and walks into the room pulling me behind him.

And in that room are Mandy and Lu.

I'm just frozen and confused for a moment. These are the traders that are trying to buy me?

More like rescuing me!

That sneaky fucking lizard scared me to death on purpose. He had to know that I wanted to go home.

Just when I realize the truth of things, Lu disappears. Just camouflages completely.

Then, just as Shawn pulls me away from the door, Lu is silently moving through it, his camouflage rapidly shifting. It's a disorientating blur.

And then he's gone.

Just what the hell does he think he's doing? Why come all the way here just to storm out?

What a frickin tool!

I don't consciously decide to follow him, but I'm shaking off Shawn and turning to stomp through the door without a thought.

I hear raised voices. Mandy, Sal, and Shawn are arguing behind me as I sprint toward the front door.

I get a feeling of déjà vu. This is not my first time running full-tilt down an alien hallway.

I almost run into Lu who is held at the door. Sal has coded locks to make sure his precious humans don't make a run for it.

"Hey!" I try to get his attention. Then I reach out, grab the tentacle nearest to me and yank.

He ignores me.

When Lu can't open the lock, he just launches himself against the door trying to bust out.

"Lu!" I yell at him. "Just what the hell do you think you're doing?"

He finally acknowledges me. Slumping his shoulders, all of his tentacles seem to fall limply around him as his color darkens and takes on a green tint.

I don't remember seeing green before. What does it mean?

"Gloria."

That's all he says, just my name.

"Lu," I answer him back in the same flat tone.

"I would like to leave. Do you know the code—"

"No," I interrupt him. "I don't know the code. Because I'm a prisoner here."

He startles, his eyes widening like this is news.

"I thought you had come here to rescue me. Because you care about me, and you miss me." I wave a hand at the door. "But obviously you don't. I'm sure Sal will let you out."

I turn and walk away from him because what the hell am I doing chasing this alien around again? He avoids me, runs away from me, and I just keep going after him. Why should I have to keep convincing him—?

A tentacle snakes around my calf, and I lose my balance a bit. But another wraps around my naked waist to steady me.

"I did," he says earnestly, more tentacles winding around my other leg and my arms. "I came to rescue you because I do miss you."

"Then why—"

"Salhuteck told us that you wanted to stay here, that you

did not wish to live with us anymore. He convinced Mandy, but I would not believe it." He is purring soothingly and combing one hand's claws through my hair. "Then I see you paired up with that male. Naked and hanging on him. Willingly touching him..."

I pet the tentacle circling my waist, soothing him. "You thought I'd picked him."

I hear his click, the sound that translates to an agreement. Then he's rubbing his cheek against mine, his purr rumbling through my whole body.

How did I go from arguing with him to snuggling him? It's nice, though.

"Give her back!"

I have to twist around in Lu's hold to see Shawn stomping toward us, clearly furious. Before I can respond, Lu has transferred me, no longer holding me in front of him. I'm tucked protectively behind him. I peek around his shoulder to see Sal come skittering down the hallway, his clawed feet scratching grooves into the floor as he slides to a stop behind Shawn.

They are both looking kind of terrified.

I glance up at Lu's face and see why. His coloring has changed dramatically. Bright, blood-red darted with black stripes. And his face— I thought he had just two fangs, but now I see that he has eight dagger-sharp fangs bared as he rises to tower over Shawn and Sal like the horrifying monster he's named for.

Then Lu lets out this awful roar. It's really loud and angry. Terrifying. Sal and Shawn cower, crouching and covering their ears.

There's an *eeep* a little way down the hall and I see Mandy peeking around the corner, wide-eyed.

"She is not yours!" He snarls at them, "Do not even look at her!"

They aren't. Their eyes are down, not daring to confront—

"AND OPEN THIS BLASTED DOOR!"

Sal scurries to respond, giving wide birth, hugging the wall as he moves around us to press one clawed digit to the sensor on the lock. Keeping his gaze glued to the floor the whole time.

There is a subtle beep and then the door swings open.

Lu looks from Sal to Shawn, snarls again, and then we move out of there so fast my hair is blown back.

Before I know it, we're in a Homeworlder shuttle and Lu is prepping to launch.

As the door lowers, I see Mandy scamper out of Salhuteck's house, her loose curls a riot blowing around her head as she's yelling something over her shoulder at the two shocked men now standing in the doorway. Lu has the shuttle door open again so she can hop in.

She runs to the back of the shuttle and grabs hold of the rail because we're already lifting off.

She smiles brightly at us and says, "That went well!"

CHAPTER TWENTY-EIGHT

—GLORIA—

Lu hasn't put me down for the past hour.

I kind of like it, but I also know that I shouldn't encourage this kind of caveman behavior.

When we got back on the homeship, the door had just opened and Lu was already hauling me out and not pausing, just barreling out of the shuttle bay. We pass Ken and Seven, who were obviously waiting for us, and I hear Ken say, "Greetings —" But Lu just snarls at him and continues on his way out of the room with me held tightly in his tentacles, high against his chest.

At least his color has calmed down. That black and red striped look was startling. He's a pale gray right now, but a little purple at the center of his chest where he's cuddling me.

We turn down a hallway that I haven't seen since my first day here when I toured the ship.

He opens a door and slides us into a room I've never been in. It's a very bare room. I think it's one of the many guest quarters on this ship. Homeworlders don't sleep in a bed, they sleep in a strange hot-tub-looking setup that's full of goo that holds their tentacles still. That's what Mandy told me. Anyway, this room has no such thing. It's definitely not Lu's personal quarters.

He settles down on the bare floor, and I can feel him relax. All of the tentacles wrapped around me ease up just a little and do a twisting caress as they move on me. He is changing color too, the gray melting into a coral pink.

"What are we doing here?"

He gazes down at me, a clawed hand combing through my hair. He's weighing his answer before he speaks.

"I want to be alone with you."

"Oh?"

"Yes." He has hit a snag combing my hair and he deftly untangles it with his claws. "I would like to talk."

I sit up straight and demand, "Are you breaking up with me?"

"I am not breaking up anyone," he answers. He looks a little bewildered.

"Okay, well, what do you want to talk about?"

"I want you to tell me how you feel about living on this ship with us. How do you feel about me?"

"So you just want me to put it all out there? Bare my soul?"

He shrugs the tentacles that aren't holding me. "This does not transla—"

"You want to know all about my feelings for you, but not tell me if you have feelings for me?"

"I have told you. I said to you that I am obsessed with you. That I find you gorgeous and your scent—"

"You're right, I remember now."

His colors all fade a little bit. "You forgot?"

"No. No," I reassure him. He looks like a kicked puppy, all wide, sad eyes. "I've just been through a lot today. My thoughts are scattered."

He nods. "Understood."

"Okay. I like living here on this ship. I want to stay and help out with rescuing humans and putting together a sanctuary, so they don't have to go through what I did when I was returned after being abducted. I like—"

He interrupts, "I want to know if you left on purpose. Did you leave because of me, because of what we did?"

"No!" I turn to face him fully. "I didn't!"

"Then how did he sneak you off that station? It seemed like you must have cooperated, otherwise how—knock-out gas does not work on humans."

"He suffocated me. I followed him into a storage room—I know that was dumb—but he closed me up in there and somehow took all the air out. I thought I was dying."

Lu snarls, startling me into silence. When he sees my reaction, he quiets himself then resumes his comforting purr. "Apologies. It is just—that is very dangerous, what you are describing."

"I know, right? I need to go back to that station and give him a piece of my mind, the kidnapping bastard!"

He combs my hair some more and says, "I will assist you."

I remember how cowed Sal and Shawn looked when Lu roared at them. That was satisfying to witness. "Okay, you can help."

I relax into his chest. He is much bigger than me. Like, I guess I get distracted by the tentacles I hadn't really taken in how huge Lu is. I'm not a small girl, but I could sprawl out on this dude like a bed. It makes me feel small and safe and taken care of being snuggled by him. Add that to the rumbling purr and the hair petting and I just feel so cozy.

I don't notice that I fall asleep on Lu, but I wake up to loud knocking on the door.

"*Glor—eee—ah!*" Mandy yells from the other side. "We have a situation!"

"What?"

"Are you decent? Can I come in?"

"No."

Mandy does an exaggerated gasp. "So you two are doing it? Like right now?"

"No!"

Ken says, "They were sleeping." From the other side of the door.

"Quiet you! How would you know?"

"Should I quiet or answer?"

"Ugh! Never mind! Gloria, get dressed and come out here!"

I respond with, "I would, except I don't have any clothes in here."

"Oh, right." There is a momentary pause and then she asks Ken, "Can you go get Gloria some clothes from the storage bay?"

I don't hear his answer, but Mandy says to me through the door, "Okay, you stay in there and I'll tell you what's going on."

"Alright."

"Sal has reported Lu to the Intergalactic-whatever of Planets. I can't remember what they're called! Anyway, Sal is being a fucking snitch and trying to get your boyfriend arrested!"

"Oh, my God!"

"Right? And it's such bullshit too because the Federation doesn't condone slavery, so Sal can't accuse him of stealing his kidnapped human slave."

I try to stand, but I'm still wound up in tentacles.

"What is Sal saying then? What did he report?" Lu isn't letting me loose, if anything he's holding me tighter and nuzzling his cheek against the top of my head as a few of the tentacles start to do this kind of pulse thing where he's caressing me while gripping me.

"He's claiming that Lu abducted you from Earth to start with! And he says that he had rescued you, but Lu stole you back and is holding you hostage!"

"That lying mother-fucker!"

"Exactly!"

"So what are we going to do?"

Lu hasn't said anything. He is wholly unconcerned as he pets and nuzzles me. His coloring is a luminous, glowing pink. If pink equals happy, then this is the happiest I've ever seen him.

Why isn't he worried about getting arrested?

"Well, that's what I wanted to talk to you guys about. We have an order that Lu is supposed to present himself to some 'Ruling Body' for judgement within three days. There's also a request for you and me to testify about our abductions. But Seven has suggested that we could speak with Sal and have him drop the charges."

This whole time she's talking, I'm trying to keep quiet because a tentacle that had been tightly wrapped around my leg has inched up, constricting, and caressing my thigh, and now it has reached—

"I don't want to talk to Sal, but that seems to be our best option and it's probably what he is counting on, the fucker."

Mandy is on a rant now, so as long as I keep quiet, she probably won't even notice that—

"Seven thinks it might be Shawn behind this whole business. Like, if Sal really cares about Shawn he might be doing all of this to try and keep him happy."

Lu has brought a rough palm to the back of my neck, his claws resting against my throat and jaw as he holds me still. I'm like putty. He's—I know he can tell what turns me on by how I smell. He knows what works. He's doing everything so slowly though. The tentacle at my upper thigh hasn't actually crossed the line. I want it to though and I find myself trying to grind down, trying to get—

"Lu, what do you think?"

"I think"—as Lu is talking that slow tentacle moves along the seam of my pussy—"that Seven is right." He spears the very tip up through my folds to caress my clit. When I gasp, he fills my mouth with another tentacle to help me keep quiet. I flashback to that time we were hiding at the beach house, and he shut me up by wrapping a tentacle around my face and I bit him. I consider biting him now. Not hard, but a little nip. I don't do that. Instead, I lick him, moving my tongue over the delicate cups on the underside of the tentacle and applying suction.

His whole body shudders. I swear, his eyes roll back in his head for a moment.

"Okay, I'll have Seven comm him and invite him to chat," Mandy says agreeably. I've completely lost the thread of this conversation. Another tentacle rubs over my whole pussy, the cups bumping against every sensitive area. Not just my pussy, but between my cheeks, too, and it's sensory overload. How did my legs end up spread open, offering everything up to this alien? Is he doing that, restraining me with his tentacles or did I position myself so lewdly without realizing it?

"I'm sure he's waiting for the call. We'll probably be able to get this over with tomorrow—oh, thanks Ken."

Lu has managed somehow to move behind me—or turn me around? It's just with all the tentacles, being held and touched in so many different ways at once, I can't keep track. He's still gripping my nape, claws digging in just a tiny bit as he feeds more of that tentacle into my mouth forcing me to open wider, take more of him as he purrs and nuzzles the side of my face.

I hear Ken talk quietly to Mandy, I can't understand what he's saying, and I don't care.

"Oh!" Mandy says, startled by whatever Ken told her. "Well, I'll just leave these clothes here for you, Gloria. Come to the cafeteria when you're—um—ready. Okay?"

The tentacle that had been rubbing my pussy changes course and it stiffens and twists inside. I immediately clamp down on it, but it keeps moving inside me, giving me more, too much. There's a stinging stretch and—

"You are so open for me," Lu says in my ear. "You want this so badly."

I draw a desperate breath through my nose as I make an inarticulate noise around—and oh, he's caressing the tips of my breasts with those cups and applying suction to my clit. He's just not letting up. I'm going to—

"It is deviant how you want to be penetrated not only here," he fucks into my pussy with a bit of force, "but also here." The tentacle in my mouth withdraws only to spear back in. "I like this." I can tell. He's purring so strongly it's vibrating my body everywhere he's touching me. "Can you take more for me? Open more?"

I don't get to answer, he just goes ahead. The grip on my thighs pulls my legs open even further as he pushes me to take more. In my mouth, in my pussy. This is more than sex, it keeps ratcheting up in intensity, and I—

"And what about..." A tentacle tip brushes against my ass, applying the slightest pressure to that opening.

I'm coming. Immediately, overwhelmingly. The tidal wave of sensation that has been building in me breaks and I'm shuddering. I think I might be spasming. Maybe I bite down on the tentacle in my mouth, I don't know. I can't keep track of my own body and my own feelings. I've completely given myself over.

As I recover, all limp muscles, and gasping breaths, he's removed all of his hands and tentacles from me, save one that is wrapped around my waist. It pulls me up to stand and then turns to push me against the wall, squishing my breasts, and I have to turn my face, so my nose doesn't hit. One knee is grasped and pushed up and away and I'm lifted so the foot touching the floor is up on tip-toe and then leaves the floor entirely as I feel the pressure of his alien cock prodding against my over-sensitive pussy. As he fucks into me, I feel myself flutter around him and then grip tightly as he works and pushes, forcing as much of himself into me as he can.

"Tell me," he growls, and that clawed hand is back on my nape, "you want this."

"I do!" I gasp as he pulls out just the slightest bit giving himself room to slam back into me, forcing me to take even more of him.

"You need me." Now he's picking up the pace, working toward his own climax. But I want—I might—

"Tell me. Say that you need me. That you would never leave —"

"I do—I wouldn't, ever—I—"

And I'm coming again, and he fucks me through it until he's coming, too. I swear I can feel that alien cock that I still haven't seen pulse as he comes.

I'm a limp noodle plastered against this wall, shivering, and gasping for breath.

This is the best, most intense sexual experience of my life. I feel—

I can't even.

Leave him? Never. Not ever.

CHAPTER TWENTY-NINE

—LU—

When Gloria is recovered and dressed, she tries to flee. Again.

The first time I mated her, she fled my presence and then disappeared from the space station. This was my mistake. I know that she likes me following her, and she likes me picking her up and holding her close to me. enough with doubts. Enough waiting for her to seek me out, to tell me what our relationship is, to show me human mating protocols.

She is mine. We are together. I will keep her close from now on.

So when she is dressed and she turns to leave with a human hand wave of farewell, I grab her hand.

I pull her back toward me and she allows it, she bares her flat teeth at me in a charming human smile.

When most beings, sentient, or animal, bare their teeth it is a threat. 'Look at my sharp fangs. Stay away.' But with humans, it seems to be the opposite. She seems to be signaling 'I am harmless and cute.'

"I need to go to the cafeteria," she says.

"I will accompany you."

She is agreeable but objects to me carrying her. This leads us to a compromise of a human mating custom, holding hands.

When two humans hold hands as they walk it is probably very easy for them, but I have some difficulty doing it. I have to stay close enough to do the handclasp but keep my tentacles from tripping Gloria. I move all of my tentacles to one side and that works but is still awkward.

I wish she would allow me to simply carry her everywhere.

As we are making our way to the cafeteria, we encounter another problem. Princess Peach comes trotting up beside us and then starts running and jumping around me in circles. Seeming to delight in nearly bumping into each of my tentacles.

When we finally reach the cafeteria, we find Mandy with a fresh marker sitting at a clean table with Ken. She twirls the implement, ready to mark up this table when she sees us. This is table number three that she has decorated with her planning, the first two having been marked up with our Saving Gloria plans. Instead of cleaning off her markings when she is done, Mandy coated them in a permanent sealant. For Posterity, whatever that means.

"Clearing. Lu's. Name," she says, writing boldly along the edge. She decorates these symbols with underlines and pointy shapes. At length, she continues, "Okay, I'm going to be real with you guys. Things don't look good. We don't have a lot of evidence. Since I was the one that picked you up, Gloria, there's no log of you agreeing to come. It looks bad that Lu was all camouflaged, stalking you so many times and then turned off the camera when you two were intimate."

She looks from Gloria to me and then looks down to where we're still doing the handholding.

"The video that Sal sent us shows Lu in a very negative light." She points her marker at me accusingly. "Very. Negative."

"Okay," Gloria answers, "but won't they take my word when I tell them what happened?"

"Ideally they would. But I'm not going to count on it because Shawn has been teaching these alien cops about human psychology, with a focus on Stockholm Syndrome."

I do not know what this means, but it enrages Gloria. She yanks her hand away from mine and yells, "That fucking tool!"

This is a very strange expletive. It translates to breeding—

implement? Very strange.

"I know!" Mandy responds in equal outrage. "He is such a douche!"

Why are all human expletives to do with breeding, genitals, and such? It is so jarring. I do like hearing how negatively they both feel toward Shawn though. I admit that I was concerned to see Gloria so close with him at Sal's residence. Knowing that she does not hold any warm feelings toward him is a relief.

Mandy brings the conversational focus back. "Anyway, so Sal and Shawn have managed to frame everything in the worst possible light. This could have some really bad, far-reaching repercussions."

"Like what?" Gloria asks.

"Well, it's been a few centuries that Homeworlders have been isolating themselves and reproducing using breeding facilities, not hosts. If Sal brings it to light that Seven and I had kids in the old way, it could be a problem. Like, for all Homeworlders."

I had not considered this. We are no longer citizens of Homeworld Two, but that does not mean that our actions have no effect on them.

"And" Mandy continues, "if Sal and Shawn succeed at making us human women look like mentally incompetent Stockholm cases, then Earth's situation might come into question."

We all three look at Mandy in confusion. What situation?

"I set up that multi-planetary defense system, right? And I hired Oh'teck to mind it. I'm basically responsible for the guardianship of Earth right now."

Gloria is suddenly scenting of alarm.

"I wasn't elected. I'm not a leader on Earth. If anybody looks into this, anybody with authority or power to challenge it, I'll be deposed. I wouldn't even fight it because I don't have an argument for why I'm the one guarding Earth. Anyway, if anyone bothers to check, nobody, no government on Earth would support my presumption either."

This situation is a lot worse than I thought. I had assumed that I was the only one being threatened and if I had to, I could just take Gloria and flee to some uninhabited sector. Only as a last recourse. But I am not the only one in danger here. Home-worlders, humans, and who knows who all else.

"So what's the plan?" Gloria asks. "Do we need to assassinate Sal or what?"

Mandy smiles brightly at her. "Not just yet! But I like your attitude. First," she starts scribbling in Earth symbols on the table, "we send a polite message asking to meet and discuss this situation before things escalate. As badly as this could go for us, it could go equally bad for Sal. He is a known slaver, from a planet that condones and traffics in the sale of sentient beings. They are bound to have enemies just waiting for a political dust up."

Everybody nods. It has always been strange to me that Seereechees are treated one way for engaging in slavery, but the lizard people of Salhuteck's world are treated another way. Even we were willing to trade with Sal, but not Seereechees. Why is that?

"There are some things that Sal wants that we can use as leverage." She draws a tiny circle on the table and begins to write next to it. "First, he has approached me a few times about wanting to have dibs on Earth-Human Art." Another dot is down under the first. "Secondly, he's asked about access to Earth. Thirdly, we all know that he's looking for a woman for Shawn."

"You can't be serious!" Gloria argues. "We can't, under any circumstances, trade a human woman to Sal!"

"Of course not. But what we can give him is access to the humans we rescue. If one of those women likes Shawn and doesn't mind living on that planet and just wants to give herself over to that whole situation. I wouldn't interfere." She holds a palm up when Gloria makes a noise. "I'm going to warn them. I won't let them be tricked. But Shawn stays with Sal willingly, it's possible that another human might too."

Gloria scowls mutinously. "Sal lied to me. Tricked me into thinking I was in danger of being handed off to some unknown human-buying aliens, when he knew it was you. He tricked Lu into reacting the way he did! I wouldn't have been clinging to Shawn that way, giving an impression like—anyway, this is all a manipulative set-up, and I don't want to give into Sal on anything."

"Sweetie, we have to compromise somewhere. We can't be the ones to instigate violence. We need to figure out a way to work with Sal."

"NO!" I wrap a tentacle around Gloria, trying to soothe her because she's getting very worked up. She ignores me. "We need to neutralize Sal somehow. If we give into his threats at all, he'll just keep coming back for more. We need to kill him. Then we take Shawn and drop him off on Earth. That's what he told me he wants."

"He said the same kind of thing to me. I don't believe him," Tiny replies firmly. "Even if he really does want to go back to Earth, he won't go with us, not willingly. He's prejudiced against Homeworlders."

Gloria starts to object, but Tiny cuts her off again, "And we aren't killing Sal. I have dealt with him in good faith for a long time. I need to actually speak with him about this situation first before we take any extreme steps."

Tiny takes a visible breath, calms down a moment then explains, "We weren't accepted into the Trader's Guild. We have no support from anybody. Until we have some kind of intergalactic standing as a people, humans should not go out assassinating trade partners, starting shit and making trouble. That shouldn't be the first impression the universe has of us, okay?"

Gloria says nothing. She glares defiantly at the floor.

"Honestly, I don't give a shit about Sal, but how can I move forward with my plans? Rescuing humans, starting a sanctuary, keeping Earth safe? How can we do any of that if we are embroiled in a violent conflict with Salhuteck's people?"

Gloria huffs, then agrees, "Okay, so we won't kill him first thing. But I want you all to understand that he's not our friend. He's a threat to us. I don't agree with giving him access to any of those things you listed. As the only other human on this ship, I feel like I should have some say in looking out for human interests."

Tiny adds some more markings to the table and when Gloria sees them, she visibly relaxes.

"Alright, if we can't compromise on any of these issues, how are we going to negotiate with Sal?" Ken asks tentatively. He looks a little shell-shocked. I think all this talk of murdering Sal is bothering him.

Gloria sits up and claps both her hands together in front her then declares, "I have an idea."

CHAPTER THIRTY

—GLORIA—

We set up our meeting with Salhuteck and Shawn. Sal demands that we let him bring a whole gang of bodyguards on the ship. Maybe he suspects that we would consider murdering him outright?

I don't know, but since I definitely am considering it, the bodyguards are kind of understandable.

Mandy countered that if he has bodyguards, we'll need some too, and it will take us a day to hire them. he'd have to rescind his accusations because we wouldn't have time to hire bodyguards, meet with Sal and then still show up before the Governing Body all within two days.

I was impressed by her gumption. Asking to drop the charges before we've even negotiated?

But he did! We even got confirmation directly from the governing body that Lu did not have to show up. They still want Mandy and me to show up in person to testify about our abductions though. She put that off for another two weeks.

In the meantime, we've put my plan into motion. I've decided that what we really need is good PR. Human stuff is super popular. A lot of the art that Mandy made, and Sal sold has humans in it and aliens are just charmed by how bald and soft and adorable we are. I've decided that being more present in the universe and actually interacting with all of these Earth-Human fans would be in our best interests. These aliens should know a little bit about humans before they hear all of Shawn's Stockholm Syndrome slander.

Mandy had shown me the social media platform and it was nothing impressive at all. It looks like a very bare combination of Instagram and eBay. You can't see any stats on it. There's no way to tell how many views and shares there are and there are no likes. So, just comments.

The first video we do is the Hokey Pokey. I decided to start really simple to test the waters. the video is Mandy and me with matching outfits doing the right hand in, right hand out. Then Peach came in and danced around when we did shake it all about. Then Ken walks by and we try to get him to do right foot in, right foot out but then look down at his tentacles, we look at each other, and burst out laughing. Ken turns half of his tentacles purple and shakes them about.

That's it. It was a lot of work to make it look casual when it was actually totally choreographed, but we pulled it off. And at the end of the video, I had Mandy say, "Comment to let us know if you want to see more videos!"

And then we included the file for Earth-Human-English with the video post.

It was a hit! There aren't a whole lot of people on this intergalactic social media, but Ken says that pretty much anybody who leaves their home planet is on it.

We got a whole lot of comments asking for more human dance instructions. Ken had to translate all of them because they were written in a galactic-standard language and written language doesn't translate with our ear-cuff translators.

Next, we did the chicken dance, teaching it to Ken and him exaggerating all of the moves with his tentacles. Then Gangnam Style and Macarena. At that point we were saving drafts to upload over the next few weeks. Surprisingly, Ken excelled at some of the dances. The Whip and the Nae Nae especially.

I'm really hoping that with all of this media exposure, evidence of us having fun with Homeworlders, and not being held prisoner, it'll be harder for Shawn and Sal to spread their Stockholm Syndrome rumors.

This morning, Ken and I did a quick interview with Mandy as she painted a new mural. It's a great big field of poppies with a sleeping Toto and an Emerald City far in the background.

Then Mandy talked for a moment about what she missed on Earth, like food and music. Would she like to go back to live there? No, never!

I'm glad that my experience with YouTube and TikTok is useful. Sometimes I don't feel like I pull my own weight around here, but most of the work requires an implant to interphase with the ship.

The only concern I really have is that we could attract the wrong sort of attention by accident. Kind of like I already did back on Earth. When I think back about that now, I get so pissed. Those men's rights activists managed to stay completely anonymous while they ruined my life. Zero repercussions for them. Well, except for the two Lu killed. That was a pretty harsh repercussion. On one hand, I feel bad about that. But on the other hand, anybody who is kidnapping and assaulting someone deserves what they get, right?

Anyway, I don't want to attract any alien stalkers or kidnappers. I talked with Mandy about it, and she agreed to hire full-time security for our ship.

It's been fun though. Alien social media is a clean slate where no trends have ever happened before. I'm trying to remember everything that's come and gone on TikTok and Instagram. Everything that's played out and boring is new here.

"So, we need to set up a meeting area. We can't use the cafeteria." Mandy says, like an hour before the meeting. We're just hanging out in the storage bay riffling through the clothes.

"What? Why not?" I ask, holding a summer dress up to my body. It's a little big, but if I belt it...

"Because of the table. I wrote out our whole negotiation strategy on the table."

"Huh." Shawn is going to be there, and he can read English just fine, it is a concern. "Did you seal it?"

She nods.

"Okay then, let's go paint over it. We'll remove the paint later and you'll still have your notes."

"That'll work! Let's get going. I need to stop by my storage room to get the paint."

I don't pretend to understand why Mandy writes on the tables. Or why she wants to preserve the notes after she's done. Creative types don't always make sense, you know?

Two guards are following us everywhere we go. They are only following closely for today. When we don't have company on the ship, they are just going to have one guard assigned to a security alcove.

The guards were a deal. Mandy was able to hire a whole pride. It's a family group of those blue-lion-looking aliens. One male with a big bushy mane like earth lions and six women. The women are all tall, strong, and fierce-looking, but beautiful, too, with their sleek blue fur and big round ears on top of their heads.

I had assumed when I heard about their group that the guy was in charge, but he isn't. One of the women, the oldest one, R'Feerah is the boss. We barely ever see the guy at all, he isn't part of the guard rotation, and he just stays on their ship which has been traveling with us since yesterday.

I tried to include one of these bodyguards in our videos, but they all refused. They are not entertainers. I guess I can respect that.

By the time we get done painting over the notes on the table, Salhuteck arrives with Shawn, a personal assistant, and three bodyguards. Everyone in his group is a lizard-person type of alien except for Shawn. And Shawn is wearing clothes. It's a kilt and a shirt that seems to be made up of wide straps crisscrossing each other. This is the first time I've seen him clothed.

Everybody greets each other with different versions of "Good Greetings". On our side, it's me, Mandy, Ken, Lu, and two of our blue lion-people bodyguards.

Then there's an awkward silence. Our plan was to wait for Sal to make his demands and accusations first and then respond with counter demands and accusations. But he doesn't say anything.

Finally, Mandy breaks the ice by asking, "What can we do for you, Sal?"

He makes a clicking noise, looks at Shawn who shrugs, then he asks, "What do you mean?"

Mandy straightens and replies, "You've slandered us to the Intergalactic Governing Body, made unwarranted threats and allegations. You had my friend here kidnapped." She gestures toward me. "I thought of you as an esteemed trade partner, Sal. I thought we had respect for each other. But now—I just don't know. I want to put this all behind us, though. tell me what I can do for you."

The whole time Mandy is talking, Sal's tail is moving back and forth across the floor in an agitated display, but he waits patiently for her to finish before he responds, "I did not have anyone kidnapped—"

"Yes, you fuckin' did!" I interject.

Mandy holds a palm up. "Let him explain."

Sal continues, "It is a rescue operation. I run many of them and not just for humans. My agent did not expect an unaccompanied human to wander into the store. He might have reacted with haste—"

"That's a lie! Why not let me go home if it was a mistake?"

"You never said that you wished to return."

Mandy whips around to look at me all wide-eyed. "You didn't tell him to return you?"

"I—" I think back. "I'm sure I did."

"I knew you were unhappy in our care," Salhuteck concedes. "But Shawn told me about the Stockholm Syndrome that human victims suffer at the hands of kidnappers. I assumed you needed time to recover."

I shake my head at them all. "This is all getting twisted. My translator was stolen. I was suffocated, then transported, changing hands three times with people who I couldn't understand and who didn't seem to understand me. Then he," I gesture to

Shawn, "told me that you gave me to him as a gift. You took my clothes—" As I'm speaking a tentacle has wrapped tightly around my waist and I feel Lu crowding against my back, growling.

Sal turns to Shawn and asks, "You told her this?"

"It's what you said," Shawn answers flatly.

"I certainly did not!"

"You said, 'Thr'shteff brought her. She is for you.'"

"To care for! To help! Not to own!"

"Shawn," Mandy interjects. He looks toward her. "Are you living with Sal willingly?"

"I..." He shakes his head as though clearing it. "Well..." He can't seem to answer.

Mandy turns to Sal.

"I have heard you called a slaver many times. I equated this word with what Seereechees do and what humans have historically done to each other. The word 'slave' is loaded, and it never jived right with yours and Shawn's situation. I've seen you offer Shawn opportunities to leave your household."

The atmosphere in here keeps getting tenser.

Mandy continues, "Tell me plainly. What do you plan to do with the humans you "rescue"? If you aren't enslaving the people in your care, why the leashes, chains and collars?"

Sal's tail is lashing back and forth with force now and his assistant must move back and give him room.

"I plan to give rescued humans sanctuary in my home. The same sanctuary I offer any beings in my care. That is what the adornments you are describing mean, that the individual is in my care and their well-being is my responsibility. It means that their actions are also my responsibility."

I look at Shawn who is staring at Salhuteck, mouth agape.

"Is that how it is, Shawn?" I ask, disbelieving.

Shawn starts to shake his head, but then we all notice a hazy fog rising from the floor. What the—

Our bodyguards all have masks that they are fastening over their muzzles, covering their noses and mouths. Only our bodyguards, not Sal's.

I feel Lu slide away from me, his tentacle falling from my waist. Ken and all the lizards are sliding to the floor as Mandy, and I look at each other.

This is an attack. It must be the knock-out gas that doesn't affect humans.

I look at our bodyguards who at least were smart enough to have those masks, but instead of looking around to figure out what is causing this, where the threat is coming from, they're looking at Mandy and me in a very focused way.

Then they grab us. Christ, these bitches are strong. I'm just snatched up and thrown over a furry shoulder. My screams, kicks, and punches have no effect as I'm carried to a shuttle and tossed in a crate.

Dammit to hell, I'm being kidnapped again!

CHAPTER THIRTY-ONE
—GLORIA—

So Salhuteck screwed us over with his dumb-ass. Reporting Lu for kidnapping an uncontacted, sentient being and then trying to rescind that report is suspicious as hell and was a red flag to the authorities. Especially since Sal himself has a reputation.

And our own bodyguards were actually bounty hunters. Totally scammed us into hiring them so they could wait until all of their marks, Sal, Lu, Seven, Ken, and all us humans were together. That's cold-blooded. In a twisted way, I have even more respect for these blue lion-women now.

They're trying to be nice now that they've captured us. Offering us snacks and stuff. Reassuring us that everything will be alright, and we'll soon be returned to our planet and our abusers will pay for their crimes. It's annoying because it's so obvious that they have no idea what is going on. How could they have hung around with us on our ship and for a day and a half and still believe that we're abused captives?

When Mandy worries about her babies being left alone, we get a sneer and a curse about "void-sent Homeworlder spawn" and reassurance that two bounty-hunters are minding the ship, our pet, and our "spawn" until this situation is resolved.

This is bad.

How are they going to resolve the situation? What are they planning to do with Mandy and Seven's kids if he's being imprisoned and we're being returned to Earth?

When we arrive at a space station, Mandy, Shawn, and I are released from our individual crates and escorted directly to "the proceedings". It's a rather small room with a raised platform on one side with a long table on it. Behind a table, sit a bunch of serious-looking aliens. It has the same feel as a courtroom on earth, but smaller and less seating.

As soon as the first judge asks a question though, Mandy doesn't even let him finish because she is freaking the fuck out.

I understand the feeling. Like, I'm worried about my dog, but Mandy has kids, helpless little alien hybrid babies that are totally defenseless.

She won't listen or respond to anything. All she wants is to get back to her kids. She keeps saying so loudly, repeatedly, talking over everyone else.

I hear one of the aliens on this panel of judges mutter "felptrig spawn". I don't know what that means, Mandy sure seems to and calls him an ugly motherfucker which he takes as a very literal accusation.

The rude one looks like one of the villains from Star Wars. With spikes on his head, claws, and fangs. Instead of being black and red like the Star Wars character though, he's white and mint green, with flat pearly-white eyes.

He's an ugly bastard, inside and out.

The rest of the panel is made up of a mix of aliens. Cat aliens, lizard aliens, little fairy aliens.

And one giant woman with wings and horns.

"You can't keep us here you fucking alien bastards!" Mandy is yelling. "Who the fuck—"

"Female—" one of the judges tries to interject.

"Don't fucking female me!"

The lion-woman judge motions toward someone behind us and it's a lion-guy. She talks quietly with him for a second, then they both look toward Mandy and talk some more. Then lion-guy grabs Mandy's arm and tells her he's going to return her to her spawn.

"Children," she corrects. "They aren't fucking animals!"

He nods, murmurs agreement, and escorts her from the room.

That leaves just Shawn and me and this panel.

"Shawn Christianson of Earth please identify yourself for the record," Blue Lioness judge instructs.

"That's me," he confirms.

"And Gloria Navarro of Earth. Please confirm your identity."

"Yeah, that's me."

"Acknowledged. You have both been remanded into the custody of this panel by the Intergalactic Order of Federated Planets in accordance with the Articles of Reconciliation. Here you will give testimony about the events of your abduction, your imprisonment, any abuse or assault you have suffered and who caused said suffering. You will then be escorted back to your planet of origin if you so choose. If you choose not to return to your planet of origin, you will be granted refugee status in all planets and guilds under the Intergalactic Order. Do you understand this process as I have explained it to you?"

Shawn and I look at each other. I don't think he understands what's going on any more than I do.

"What about the right to remain silent?" he asks politely.

"Is this a right granted to Humans of Earth during legal proceedings?" one of the judges asks.

Shawn looks at me, and I shrug. I'm not sure. I think it's an arrest thing, not a court thing. But there is the fifth amendment. Like not being required to testify against yourself? It's kind of the same thing?

"Yes," Shawn says with confidence.

"Then you are hereby allowed the right to silence."

All the judges look at me.

"I would like to report an abduction and name the one who is responsible for my suffering," I say.

Shawn looks worried. He probably thought I would be silent.

The winged judge makes a motion with her hand and says, "Please do."

"I was abducted from my homeship by agents of the Intergalactic Order of Federated Planets. I was emotionally harmed, insulted, and threatened."

All the judges start grumbling at once.

"Highly improper!"

"Backward barbarian."

"The nerve!"

"I demand to be returned to my homeship, together with my mate, Lu of Homeworld Two," I say loudly.

Then the whole proceedings break down and one of the judges attempts to dismiss everyone saying we'll reconvene tomorrow, but I loudly object to that.

"Where should we go until tomorrow? Are we still being detained or are you all going to return us to my ship?"

There is a chaos of alien languages yelling back and forth as all these judges start arguing with each other about whether we should be detained or not.

I interrupt loudly again, "If I am not being charged with a crime, I should be free to go!"

At that point, the lion-guy who had escorted Mandy away came back. He was instructed to escort Shawn and me to our ship, but then bring the ship to this station and escort us back to this room tomorrow. He was also told to "continuously read" us, whatever that means.

I find out what it means when I'm thirsty and he brings me a drink without me saying anything. Then I start trying to think of ways we could escape and if we do how would I get Lu, Seven, and Ken back.

"You cannot," the guy answers my unspoken thoughts. "And my name is Kenthack, not Lion-Guy."

Kenthack is actually an alright dude. He doesn't lock us up or make annoying-ass comments. Out of everyone we've dealt with today, he's the okay-est. But I can't forget that he's also our jailer. Our telepathic jailer.

Shawn is quiet. Not talking with me or anyone. He's taking this right to remain silent thing a little far.

"So, Kenthack," I say. "What do I have to do to get all my

friends released and the intergalactic order out of our business? Nobody has committed any crimes—"

"What about when this one's owner kidnapped you and held you captive?" He points a clawed thumb toward Shawn,

"That was a misunderstanding," I tell him. If he's reading my thoughts, he's aware of that. "And it's rude to snoop through my memories."

Kenthack huffs at me, but he looks—embarrassed? Have I struck a nerve?

"Intentions do not matter. Accidentally kidnapping a sentient being is just as illegal as intentionally doing so."

"This is not evidence," I tell him. "You can't violate someone's privacy like this for the sake of prosecution."

He nods and says, "That's true. I am not going to testify about anything. Just letting you know that you are lying to me and yourself if you say that your friends haven't committed a crime. Your Homeworlder friends violated the laws of their planet and the IOFP in their treatment of you and that other female."

I search my memories. How have they treated us that is illegal? Is it the sex? Like, is interspecies sex illegal?

"Please do not," Kenthack shudders.

"What?"

"Do not think of such intimate things."

Oh, so he doesn't have a choice about reading my mind. And he doesn't want me thinking about—

"Please, stop."

Well, snooping telepaths deserve what they get as far as I'm concerned. I make it a point to remember and relive every intimate moment I've had with Lu. I haven't had a ton. I remember the few sex partners I've had on Earth for good measure. Once I even had a threesome—

"Humans are disgusting."

I laugh evilly and work on remembering any porn I've seen. It's not like I watch a ton of it, but—

"Are all Earth-Humans so deviant?" he demands.

This is fun. I keep it up for the rest of the trip.

When we finally make it home, there is some tension between Kenthack and the bodyguards/bounty hunters still occupying our ship. The first one we encounter hisses loudly at him. He does this snarl sound in return and spits. He spits on the floor right next to her.

Rude. What's that all about?

I don't waste time. I quickly show Shawn and Kenthack to guest quarters and then go find Mandy who's hanging out with the kids and Peach in her room. It's a strange experience because I'm used to Seven lurking around whenever I'm around his kids. It's a thing with Homeworlders that they feel driven to "guard" their young. It makes me kind of sad not to see Seven here guarding. And then I think of how Lu isn't here on the ship either.

This sucks. We might not be able to get the guys back. What's going to happen with them? Where are they right now?

I have a really hard time getting to sleep and it seems like I'm only asleep for an hour when we must get up and get ready to leave again.

Mandy doesn't have to return, just me and Shawn. They probably don't want her yelling the room down again.

The "proceedings" are in a completely different room and circumstances now. The lion alien and the winged alien are the only ones here. They are sitting at a rectangular table waiting for us to join them. Shawn and I sit in the seats across from them. Kenthack leans over the other lion-alien and talks quietly with her for a moment, then leaves.

"Good greetings," the winged-alien says.

"Greetings," I reply.

Shawn maintains his silence.

"We would like to discuss admitting your planet into the Intergalactic order—"

"That's a bad idea," I interrupt.

"We have admitted R-Class planets before. Earth will not be harmed, I assure you."

I laugh. "It's not Earth I'm worried about."

"Oh? What is your worry?"

I lean onto the table and try to think for a second. Order my thoughts and plan what I should say. Then I just blurt out the truth.

"Humans are a plague. I mean, an individual human might be nice. We might look harmless and adorable. But there is one thing that humans excel at and that is breeding. A single couple can have up to twenty kids. We'd hog all the resources and drive the rest of the galaxy to extinction if given free range. You don't want to help humans leave Earth. Ever."

"But—"

I hold up my palm. "You need to rethink this. I'm sure Mandy will allow some kind of reconnaissance so you guys can learn about humans before you move ahead with any plans. It's not my place to decide the fate of Earth, but you all need to really think about it before you try to open this can of worms."

They look disgusted and it takes me a moment to realize that the phrase "can of worms" must have been translated literally.

They wait in silence for a while, then nod.

"We will reconnoiter Earth as you advise and revisit the issue of admittance later."

"Okay. Are we good to go? When will you release my mate? My crewmates?"

I'm pure bluster at this point, but they surprise me by saying, "Your crewmates are being released presently. All inquiries into the matter of your abduction have been suspended."

"Well, thanks, that's great!"

"Please relay this information to the other human. Since you will not be returning to your planet, you are automatically granted refugee status which you can maintain indefinitely."

"Okay."

The winged-alien turns her attention to Shawn.

"You can stay silent if you wish and be transported back to your planet. If you have other preferences, you will need to voice them."

He blinks once and then replies, "I don't want to return to Earth." He looks at me. "Can I stay with y'all for a bit?"

I nod. "Of course."

CHAPTER THIRTY-TWO

—LU—

One moment I am in the cafeteria, listening to Salhuteck's lies and manipulations, and the next I'm waking from cryo-sleep.

This is the second time this has happened to me, and it is not any more bearable than the first.

The cryopod has been positioned vertically against a wall. I tumble out of it to spill onto the floor before I can get my bearings.

As I lay on the floor, I look around at this very bare room. There is nothing in here except for the cryopod and myself.

What has happened?

Where is everyone? Where is Gloria?

After taking a few breaths and gaining equilibrium, I find the door. It is locked to me.

This is obviously not a ship. Even if my implant is not allowed to interface, I could tell if there were ship operations.

So this is a planet? Or a station? It is unlikely that I have been taken by Seereechees again.

There is a fogginess to my thoughts. This is a regular thing, waking from cryo with impaired cognition. As it clears, one thought comes to the foreground of my brain: Salhuteck has betrayed us. Again.

I am now in agreement with Gloria. He needs to be killed, at the very next opportunity. As soon as I escape from whatever situation this is, I will find Gloria and then we will track down Sal and his human and kill them. They are a constant threat to us.

Gloria may not want Shawn to die, and if that's the case, we can just transport him back to Earth and leave him at the mercy of their officials.

Worries keep popping into my head, pictures of what may be happening to Gloria right this instant.

There is absolutely nothing for me to do though. This is a secure room. I cannot escape until somebody opens that door from the outside. I can only hope that Gloria is in the situation as I, safely detained and not being abused in any way.

As soon as that door opens, I'm going to charge whoever is on the other side, toss them away and make an escape. I try to ready myself for this confrontation, but I do not know who may open that door.

Whoever it is though, they are holding me hostage, keeping me from my mate and they will be dealt with swiftly.

My color is darkening while I focus my thoughts on violence. I see red stripes pop up on my arm and it startles me so much that I lose that focus and they disappear.

This red coloring is new. I first experienced it at Sal's when I raged and roared at him and his human.

It seems to correspond not with a change in my biology, but a change in my—mood? Personality? I am willing to do terrible violence now and my color reflects that propensity.

It is disconcerting.

There is a quiet whirring sound. That indicates that the door is about to open.

I crouch, ready to spring at whoever comes through.

But when the door opens, the person on the other side yells, "Lu!" and lunges at me.

It's Gloria! She's clinging to me and squeezing me. I snake a few tentacles around her, holding her so she does not fall, and look out the door.

What is going on? How is she free from imprisonment? Do

we need to run?

But on the other side of the door are Tiny, Seven, and Shawn. Shawn.

I growl at him. He glowers back at me. Whatever is going on, I am sure he had a hand in it.

I feel Gloria grab my shoulder and give it a shake. "Cut that out. We need to get out of here without any more incidents."

Cutting my growl off, I look down at Gloria's face.

She is here. Safe. We are leaving.

I deliver my best approximation of a human kiss to her forehead and say, "Agreed."

"Awww." This sound is coming from Tiny. When I glance at her, I see Seven swoop in from behind her and kiss her forehead.

She laughs at him.

Everything seems to be alright. I am glad we are not in immediate danger, but this is all very confusing.

And why is Shawn part of this group?

"Let's go." Gloria is shaking my shoulder again. "We still need to get Ken and Sal."

Moving out the door and following Tiny and Seven down the hall, I ask, "Why are we concerning ourselves with Salhuteck? Why is his human with us? They are liars and kidn—"

Gloria has her hand over my mouth silencing me. "I'll explain when we're safely back on our ship."

We retrieve Ken, who has much the same confused reaction as I did. He also growls at Shawn. He receives the same admonishment to wait for an explanation until we are gone from here.

As we continue down the corridor to find Salhuteck, I notice that we are being followed. It is one of those blue furry people. Like the bodyguards Tiny hired, only male.

Gloria notices me noticing him and says, "Don't worry about him. He's just our escort. I'll explain later."

The more we walk around collecting people, the more disorientation sets in.

Where are we? How did we come to be here? Why?

Salhuteck also being detained contradicts my theory that

this is a betrayal perpetrated by him.

Who then?

After we have retrieved everybody, we are a large group. The escort, Tiny, Gloria, Ken, Seven, Sal, Shawn, and Sal's three bodyguards. A lot of good they did. Our bodyguards were obviously useless as well.

"But—Tiny, what about your bodyguards?"

Her mouth presses into a thin line and her eyebrows lower. She looks angry. "What about them?"

"We should retrieve them—"

"No," Gloria interrupts, "They weren't detained. I'll explain later."

I nod and give her a small squeeze where my tentacle is still wrapped around her waist. To let her know that we are in agreement. I will do whatever she needs me to do.

"The shuttle is this way, friends," our escort tells us.

I hear Tiny make a disbelieving "hmmph," noise at the word friends.

"Are we not friends?" the escort asks as he guides us through multiple corridors, past many people.

"You want to be our friend, Kenthack?" Gloria asks. I do not like the familiarity. How well does she know this male?

"I thought we already were friends," he answers jovially. "We have been through much together, after all?"

"Not at all," Gloria responds.

"And you shared so many of your experiences with me. Does that not engender closeness? Friendship?"

He seems to be teasing Gloria. I do not like it.

For her part, Gloria has a confused look about her face and her scent conveys this. Understanding seems to dawn over her features and with it, embarrassment clouds her scent and colors her cheeks and neck.

"That's not what that was! I was just giving you shit!"

Kenthack gets a disgusted look on his face and says, "Please do not."

"Ugh, jeez, not literal shit—"

Tiny holds up a hand. "It doesn't matter. Thanks for your help, Kenthack."

We have arrived at the shuttle and Tiny is dismissing him.

"I must accompany you onto your homeship and ensure your safety. That is my assigned task," he responds.

"Oh, fine. Whatever."

It is a very crowded shuttle ride to our ship. Everybody is quiet, though. I wonder at Salhuteck's silence. He has not said a word since we retrieved him from his cryopod.

There is some commotion when we finally dock. Our own bodyguards wait for us.

Tiny immediately dismisses them, but they try to negotiate. Until they see Kenthack at which point they all hiss and snarl at him. He snarls and growls back and then spits at them. Or more precisely, spits on the floor in their direction.

Our former bodyguards leave the shuttle bay.

Kenthack turns to Tiny and tells her, "You should consider hiring them on permanently. That is what they wanted to discuss with you."

"But they betrayed us! Kidnapped us!"

He shrugs. "They were hired to collect a bounty and they did. They were very fair and considerate in the way they did it too."

"They called my children filthy spawn."

"I do not aim to prick your feelings, but everyone in three whole galaxies will react to your progeny thus. Homeworlders are universally reviled. Anyone who knows of them, hates them."

I squeeze Gloria and she pats my tentacle where it has remained cinched around her waist this whole time.

Not everyone hates us.

"This is just—" Tiny shakes her head. "I just can't deal with it. Gloria, you decide about the bodyguard situation. I'm done."

And then she stomps out of the shuttle bay, Seven right behind her.

Ken looks at me, then Gloria. "We do need permanent bodyguards and they come highly recommended. They do not have to like us to work for us."

"Okay," she agrees. "If that's really how things are and they're the best we could hope for then…" She waves a hand in the direction they went.

Ken follows her unspoken command and leaves, saying, "I will renew their contract."

It is now Gloria, Shawn, Sal, Sal's three bodyguards, Kenthack, and myself.

"Thanks for your help, Kenthack," Gloria dismisses him.

He gestures to Salhuteck. "This male and his entourage need to leave first. And after I depart, you should fold to an unknown point in space so that he cannot follow."

I growl, Shawn gasps, and Gloria crows, "I fuckin knew it! I told you guys he's out to get us! We can't trust them." She waves toward the whole group including Shawn.

"But you said I could stay!" This is the first I have heard Shawn speak since waking from cryo.

Sal looks at him, startled and aghast.

"Not if you're conspiring against us!" She waves toward Kenthack. "He's a mind-reader. If he says you guys are out to get us, then you are!"

"Not the human," Kenthack corrects.

We all look at Sal, but he's looking at Shawn.

"You wish to stay? You are not coming home?"

"You have always said that I could leave if I wanted to. That it's my choice. Well, I'm choosing."

Sal dips his chin in acknowledgment. "Of course. Of course, I honor your choice, Small One."

Sal snaps his clawed digits at his associates, and they all move toward their own shuttle.

"Gloria, why are you allowing Shawn to stay with us? We should send him with Sal," I advise.

Gloria shakes her head.

"But he held you prisoner. Why would you want to keep him?"

"He was a captive the same as I was. A prisoner minding another prisoner is kind of a morally gray area, I think."

I cannot believe I am hearing this from her.

"I do not want him here."

"Sorry Lu, but I already told him he could stay and I'm not going back on it. It's a big ship, you guys can just stay away from each other."

"I do not want him near you!"

"You're not in charge of who I hang out with."

This is so frustrating! How can I keep her safe if she insists on allowing this ill-behaved, untrustworthy male into her life?

Before I am aware of it, I rumble a growl.

Gloria's eyes widen and she slaps the tentacle I have wound around her.

"You struck me!" I accuse.

Why is she being like this? This is all Shawn's fault.

"You growled at me!" she yells back.

She pulls my tentacle off her waist and steps away from me.

"C'mon Shawn, I'll give you a tour."

They leave the shuttle bay.

Turning back, I see that Sal had paused his exit. He quickly resumes climbing into his shuttle and leaves with his associates.

I am left with Kenthack. Surely, he will leave now.

"Sal is not any kind of threat to you without Shawn. He was determined to acquire a human companion for him."

I tilt my head in understanding.

"And Shawn is not a threat to anybody now that he has decided to stay on this ship."

I perform a nod but realize this male does not know about human nods and so tilt my head in agreement again.

"I will be going then. Good parting, Lu."

"Good parting, Kenthack."

I am soon alone and free to track down Gloria.

CHAPTER THIRTY-THREE
—GLORIA—

I am fuming.

I dropped Shawn off at his room after a short tour. Then I grabbed a drink and a snack and after I was done with that I went to check in on Mandy and pick up Peach. When I got to her room though, I heard some noises that made me change my mind about visiting.

Really? They're already at it? We just got home.

So now I'm alone with my thoughts and my thoughts are about Lu and how difficult he is.

He doesn't actually care about Shawn being here. He just doesn't want me near Shawn. There's not a lot of us humans out here and if I want to help Shawn out and try to be his friend that's my decision. If anybody has beef with Shawn, it's me. Not Lu. And I've decided to move past it, so Lu can just deal.

Did I come all the way out here, trying to make a life for myself away from Earth just to be controlled by my alien boyfriend? No.

Mandy and I have been planning to help rescue every human we can find and the first one to ask for my help just happens to be Shawn.

And what does Lu think? Like I'm going to cheat on him or something? If I wanted to be with Shawn, I could have! I was hanging out with him, naked, alone for most of the time I was at Sal's. And nothing happened!

It just feels like Lu is accusing me of something. Like he doesn't trust me. And that's not fair. We don't have any kind of agreement, do we? Lu has never talked about us being exclusive. Not once. I have given him no reason to think I would cheat.

There's a blur of movement in my peripheral vision and I know he's stalking me again. I don't know why that makes me feel—warm? Anybody else sneakily following me around would creep me out, but not him. I'm glad that he's still seeking me out even after our disagreement.

As I move through the door to my room, it stays open a moment longer because Lu is sliding in behind me even if I can't see him. When I focus, I can make out the blurry edge of his camouflaged form.

A tentacle snakes out and quickly wraps around my waist as his color changes to his regular gray. Well, except for the tentacle that has me, that one is bright pink at the tip fading to purple then to gray where it meets the rest of his body.

"You are my mate," he says as if the words are being torn from him. "Mine."

I nod and agree, "Yes."

He crowds against me, tentacles winding around my arms and legs. My breathing picks up, heart beats a little faster. Who knew that this would be what really does it for me in bed? Being stalked and grabbed by a tentacled alien?

"There is nothing that human can do for you that I would not." He's lifting me right off the ground, pulling my skirt and shirt up as he positions me how he wants. "You do not need him."

As he nuzzles the side of my face, I nuzzle him right back and kiss his cheek. "You're right I don't need him. Only you."

He starts purring and his whole body is taking on that luminous pink color that lets me know how delighted he is with me.

"I want to try something," I tell him. "Set me down."

All of the tentacles tighten for a second and I briefly wonder if he's going to ignore me, but he does lower me to the floor. The pink color fades a little bit, but hopefully, it'll return to the same intensity in a moment.

"You know, there are all sorts of things we could do. Not just regular sex," I inform him.

"Oh?"

"Yeah. There's a thing called oral sex."

His eyes go a little wide. "You want me to mouth your—"

I wave my hand to interrupt him. "Maybe later." I kneel. "Right now I want to put my mouth on you."

His tentacles scrunch up. "But why?"

Smiling sweetly, I cajole, "I think you'll like it a lot." When he looks even more uncomfortable, I concede. "You don't have to say yes, but we could try it and stop if you don't like it."

His tentacles are still scrunched. "Why would you enjoy that?"

I give him another smile. "Remember last time? When you put one of these—" I caress the tentacle closest to me and it unscrunches. "—in my mouth? It kinda turned me on for you to do that..."

His purr picks up again.

"I would like it even more if it was your cock."

His purr stutters a little bit. "I do not have—that does not translate. You are talking about putting your mouth on my implantation arm? That would please you?"

I laugh before I can stop myself. He's such a dork.

"Yeah, but I'd rather call it a cock."

I've made him self-conscious. Maybe this wasn't a great idea. I've been curious to see what he's working with this whole time, but I didn't mean to kill the mood.

Reaching out, I touch one of his tentacles where it meets his upper body. I trace it all the way down to the tip. It's a lot longer than it seems, and it takes me a moment to follow the swirl pattern it's in resting on the floor. Then I pick it up and caress the underside. I know these cups are sensitive. I run a finger delicately around each one.

"You know octopuses, they have tentacles like these, and they can taste things with their cups."

He nods. "Yes, they have taste receptors."

"So you're tasting the floor wherever you go?"

"Yes, we keep the floors here very clean for that reason."

"And when you touch me with these, you're tasting me too?"

I feel tentacles creeping around me, winding around my waist, wrapping around my thighs as I kneel in front of him. My legs are pried open, and a tentacle rubs against my open pussy, each cup bumping and caressing sensitive areas as he purrs. "Yes. I taste you this way."

I'm squirming a little bit from the sensation, so the tentacles clamp tighter, holding me still. Another wraps around my arms, pinning them to my side as the lower tentacle changes course and spears my cunt. I'm so turned on right now, I would think it'd ease his way. But he's rough with it, filling me quickly, completely until there's a delicious, stinging stretch as he forces me to make room for him.

As he works my clit, sucking on it with the cups of yet another tentacle, I gaze up at him towering over me. Cthulhu. He's well-named. I have a feeling of offering myself up as if he really is an elder-god and I'm a sacrifice.

I'm close. If he keeps it up, I'm going to come. But I feel a nudge at my cheek. I look and, well, it's not a human cock. Like the illustration, it's wider at the base, narrow at the head. And where a human cock has a small slit, this one has a seem bifurcating the whole head, like it could split in two.

"Open," he demands. "Taste me, as you said."

Oh, that tightens something in my core, and I feel my pussy spasm around the tentacle that's still fucking me.

I open my mouth and lick him along the underside of it. His whole body shudders. Then he's feeding this very alien cock into my mouth, slowly. Pulls out and pushes back in deliberately.

A clawed hand combs through my hair and palms the back of my head as he starts to fuck my mouth in shallow thrusts.

"Careful with those teeth, little human," he huffs, then purrs. "My pretty mate, my Gloria."

He's got good coordination because he's fucking me with a tentacle as he fucks my mouth with his cock and circles my clit and oooooh—

"You please me so well. With your mouth and your cunt and this soft body." He nudges the back of my throat. "Can you take a little more for me? Yes, exactly. Just like that."

He's fucking my throat, his cock can move on its own and it's doing this twirling motion as it fucks into my throat, and I'm doing my best to breathe and swallow.

That feeling comes over me again, of offering myself up to him, for his pleasure and I grind down on the tentacle at my pussy and then I'm coming, pulsing around him in my cunt, moaning around him in my mouth. He's taken over my whole body and made it sing for him. It lasts so long, that I'm shuddering, squeezing, sucking, and grinding on him. Am I coming again? I can't even tell.

He's touching every part of me and getting rougher, his movements a little jerky. Two clawed hands holding my head still now so he can use my mouth to get himself off.

"You like this. I can smell how much it pleases you. And you taste so good. You feel—"

He grimaces, showing fangs as he comes. It's not like human cum at all. A syrupy texture and tangy, citrus flavor. Not bad, but surprising as I don't swallow quick enough and some dribbles out of my mouth. With care, he extricates himself from me, then swipes my chin and mouth with a tentacle tip.

"Swallow," he instructs me.

Wanting to please him, I lick the tip clean and swallow. His purr ratchets up and his color is a luminous bright pink everywhere.

"Humans," he says at length, "are criminally deviant. There should be a law about this kind of behavior."

"There probably is."

He picks me up and snuggles me to his chest. It's perfect. I always want to be snuggled after sex.

"You love my deviant behavior," I tell him.

He hums in agreement.

"You love me."

He combs my hair with his claws and says, "Of course I do."

"I love you too," I murmur. I can tell he hears me because I get a quick, tight squeeze from arms and tentacles.

CHAPTER THIRTY-FOUR

—LU—

The problem with Shawn took care of itself very quickly. I need not have worried.

He was on our ship for four nights. Then he woke up one morning, came to the cafeteria, and informed everyone that he had commed Salhuteck, shared our location, and he would be leaving us shortly.

"Are you guys going to try and kidnap anybody on your way out?" Gloria asked him.

He stared at the floor with his face set in a frown.

Tiny was more solicitous. "Would you like to take any clothes or—"

"He can't wear clothes at Sal's place," Gloria snickers.

"Thanks, Mandy, but I can have whatever I need made at home." Shawn answers with a stoic air.

"Home is it?" Gloria asks.

Shawn nods.

"So, are you and Sal, like, a couple?"

"No."

"C'mon," Gloria argues, "If you're not together then why are you going back to him?"

"Not that it's any of your business," Shawn explains looking from Gloria to Tiny and back, "but I've considered my options. I can be detained indefinitely on Earth. I can live here with you all." He waves a hand around to encompass Ken, Seven, and I.

"Or I can be part of some primitive refugee situation on Mars or wherever. I think Sal is my best option."

Gloria smirks, "And you miss him. Admit it."

Shawn shakes his head and huffs, not looking anybody in the eye.

"It's not like that."

Gloria laughs again.

"Oh really? So all the petting and compliments aren't you're cup of tea? All of the collars and leashes and—" She wiggles two fingers on each hand at him. "Punishments? You're not into any of that? And you're going back to him for more of that treatment anyway."

"You don't understand."

"Explain it to me."

"Gloria," Tiny interjects, "You're being a jerk. He doesn't have to explain."

"Not everyone is an alien-fucker," Shawn says heatedly.

Gloria laughs some more.

"Who said anything about fucking aliens Shawn? I certainly didn't. Obviously it's on your mind though—"

There is a notification in our implants and tablets that a shuttle has docked. Shawn turns on his heel and stomps toward the corridor.

"Bye Shawn!" Gloria yells, "Have fun!"

He waves a hand over his head but does not respond or turn around.

"Well," Tiny says at length, "as long as he's happy."

Gloria nods.

"Okay, well, what were we talking about? Rescuing people?" Tiny asks.

Tiny and Gloria want to rescue a Human from the Arana-Vora Homeworld.

Tiny seems to believe that we can just ask Baht politely to please give his human over to us. She has faith that Baht will immediately acquiesce.

This is folly.

For one thing, Arana-Vora are ruled by their females. The females never leave their home planet. If that is where this human is, then Baht will have little say in the matter.

It is said that female Arana-Vora are vicious, bloodthirsty, and incapable of rational negotiation. In the same way as the males, but worse.

This is a doomed proposition from the start. I wish we had never been alerted to this situation.

Though Tiny has divided ownership of our homeship between the five of us, control has not derived from ownership. When Tiny and Gloria decide on a course of action, that is it. It is set. It is curious to me that these weak, delicate little humans have maneuvered themselves into positions of authority.

This proposition of contacting the Arana-Vora Homeworld, possibly going there? I cannot agree with it. I will put a stop to it if it comes to that. I just need to make sure that Ken and Seven are on my side in this. Tiny and Gloria do not have implants to pilot the ship. If those of us that can pilot will not go, then that is that. I hope. Unless they think to have one of the bodyguards pilot.

"We will not survive this encounter," Ken laments, voicing my thoughts for me.

"Don't be so negative." Tiny says.

"If it's as dangerous as all that, more reason to get her out of there as soon as possible," Gloria argues, "None of these other humans are in such dire need of rescue as this one."

"We will not be able to rescue any of them if we die on that planet. You are bringing us right to them and they will devour us," Ken argues.

I watch Gloria think about that for a moment. I can almost read her thoughts, listing everything at risk. Tiny and Seven's spawn, Princess Peach, any Humans we may help in the future, and on and on.

"Maybe let's put this one to the back of the list," she says.

"What? Why?" Tiny asks.

"Well, look, who sent us this notice. It's an anonymous tip.

That's suspicious. It could very well be a trap."

"Huh," Tiny is rethinking, thank the void, "Yeah, those spider aliens are trying to get free food delivered right to their door."

They have both given in. This is a relief.

"Okay, so we'll back-burner that one pending more evidence. Which human are we going to rescue then?" Tiny asks.

Ken starts listing, "There is a group of ten humans on Risant Eight Space Station now. They are living as refugees."

"Are they safe there?" Tiny asks.

"Yes. It is a very clean space station. Well within patrolled space. It is run by a responsible and law-abiding Crimbulonian. Darfeech, I think their name is. When the situation with Humans being mistaken for pets came to light, they declared their station a safe haven for humans where owners can drop them off without any questions," Ken explains, "Next is a human that was adopted as a pet, but the ship they were on has crashed on a very inhospitable planet."

"Do we know if they survived?"

Ken shakes his head.

"Okay, we'll swing by and check on them first."

Ken nods and continues, "A human was bought as breeding stock and impregnated with crown prince's heir in Herf-Trtut, a planetary system in the far reaches of a neighboring galaxy."

"Oh my god!" Gloria says.

"She has been emancipated and granted citizenship on that planet, but perhaps we should check on her."

"We certainly will," Tiny says.

"And Oh'Teck has informed me that two humans and three cats are now living on the security station with him. He has also told me that he has reason to believe that everyone who was returned to Earth with Gloria is still being detained."

"Oh, no," Gloria says, "Those poor women! We should rescue them too!"

"How did humans and cats get on the security station though?" Tiny asks.

Ken shrugs, "Oh'Teck must have brought them there."

"Okay, if that's all—" Tiny starts to say.

"It is not," Ken interrupts, "There is a distress signal coming from Earth. From a crashed ship."

"But how could anybody crash on Earth? They can't get past our security field?" Tiny looks around at all of us. "Right? That's the whole point of it."

"Yes. A ship must have crashed before we got the security system up and they just now were able to get a signal out." Ken posits.

"Okay, alright. First, let's go check that ship that crashed on the inhospitable planet. Then we'll check on the pregnant woman. Then we'll check on Oh'Teck, the detained women and this distress signal back on Earth. Then we'll check on the refugee space station." Everybody is nodding along as Tiny lists these points of action and writes them down with flourish on the table. "Then we'll revisit this Arana-Vora situation."

I do not know what Tiny is going to make lists on now that she is covering the last clear table with her markings. Maybe she will start using a tablet as one is meant to.

Using the tentacle I have loosely wrapped around Gloria's waist I pull her close so I can nuzzle her face and breathe in her scent.

I crave Gloria's attention because she has been distracted lately. Not just with human rescue plans. She is always talking with Tiny about the human sanctuary they have under construction on a planet neighboring Earth. And the traders' guild they are planning to found. Founding a trader's guild is a project so large in scope that I do not see how it can possibly be accomplished. That is their plan though. I am going to be supportive even though I do not think it is feasible.

As she caresses the tentacle that is holding her and nuzzles me back I cannot help but bask in her attention.

She is mine, my mate. And we are together as we are meant to be. It is all that matters.

EPILOGUE
—GLORIA—

Four months later

We've hit some snags.

Our human rescue operation is not going well. Or, I guess I would say that it is not going as expected. Every single human we have tried to rescue didn't need or want help.

It started with Shawn who up and went back to Sal after just four days. Then, by the time we checked on the women being detained on Earth they had all been let free. I think Oh'Teck had something to do with it, but he's being tight lipped about it. Speaking of Oh'Teck, apparently he discovered Only Fans and ended up abducting the couple he subscribed to. And their cats. I'm really confused about how all that unfolded logistically, but from what I understand they are a thruple. I think. I'm not going to be nosy about it as long as they're all happy, and they all seem to be.

The mysterious distress signal didn't come to anything.

The human that had crashed on the inhospitable planet was alive and well with a whole pack of alien boyfriends she had acquired by accident but decided to keep. She didn't need rescuing either.

The pregnant one is involved in a custody battle for the baby she's pregnant with. She can't leave while all that is being decided. She asked us to check on her again closer to her due date.

When we checked on the refugee space station it had been through a bloodless coup. Humans and their allies had taken over the whole station. The previous director has disappeared. It is being investigated by the Governing Body. After hearing from those humans that none of them wanted to leave, we got out of there with quickness. We don't want to be sucked into that sort of drama.

Mandy has put a pause on the human sanctuary. It's pretty obvious now that nobody likes the idea of living in a sanctuary. Maybe they would if they were actually in terribly dire states, but so far all the humans we've tracked down are doing okay and pretty much living life on their own terms out here in space.

So that leaves us with the Arana-Vora planet and the human we keep hearing is still alive and trapped on there.

We can't just ignore this situation, but we also can't blunder about on a planet of vicious, bloodthirst spider people. Mandy and I keep going back and forth about it. We still don't know how reliable these anonymous reports are. If there really is a human on that planet how has she stayed alive this long? If she's still alive, maybe it's not dangerous for us to visit and check on her.

But we can't know anything for sure. That planet is closed off from the rest of the universe. No calls, surveillance, or any kind of communication at all. We've tried getting messages through, tried hiring bounty hunters, all with no results.

Mandy, Lu, Seven, Ken, and I are all in the cafeteria heatedly debating our options when our ship's communication system is pinged with a request. An unknown person who won't identify themselves is trying to chat with us.

It could be anybody, any of these humans we have been in contact with lately. I cross my fingers as we hurry to the security alcove to establish a video feed. I hope it is from the Arana-Vora planet. Please let us finally have a definitive answer about this woman's situation.

My prayers are answered when a spider guy appears on the display. I recognize what he is even though he is hunched into a ridiculous cloak. His glowing red eyes give him away.

"Greetings, Baht," Lu says breaking the ice.

We all take turns saying different versions of "greetings" to each other.

Then I get right to it. "Do you still have that woman from the Seereechee ship with you Baht? Is she alive?"

"She is," he answers, "but that is not your concern."

"It kind of is," Mandy argues.

"I have contacted you about a matter of great urgency. Much more important than human gossip."

I don't like his dismissive tone. Mandy has more patience than me because she asks, "What is the matter you're calling about?"

"There has been an unforeseen astral event."

What does that even mean?

"Speak plainly Baht," Mandy demands.

"A previously undetected rogue black hole shot through an outer arm of your galaxy two years ago," he explains slowly looking at us humans, "it has interfered with local orbits."

We all look at him dumbly. It's clear that he expected a reaction, but I am still not sure what he's saying.

"Is Earth's sun affected by this?" Ken asks.

"Not directly. Two nearby stars will collide in less than ten days though. Two days after that Earth will experience catastrophic effects."

"That doesn't make any sense," Mandy argues, "The nearest star to our system is more than four light years away. How would these effects reach Earth so soon?"

Baht looks at Mandy for a moment. At length he says, "You would like a lesson in interstellar physics?"

"Yes."

Baht stands a little taller and shrugs his shoulders, then begins, "When massive bodies collide in space, this causes a concussive fold effect."

"And what is a concussive fold?"

"It is similar to how your ship folds space to travel great distances, but on a much larger scale. Instead of a single fold, the fabric of space-time is folded violently, multiple times. Space-time itself is folded up, scrunched into a ball around this collision."

Baht looks at Mandy and she nods for him to continue.

"As quickly as this large, multilayer fold happens, it unfolds. It explodes out. Pushing time-line events that have gotten passed from one folded crest to another outward with jarring immediacy. Something you otherwise would not even glimpse for ten years is at your door in seconds. Effects that should be dampened and spaced out over time, happen in rapid succession."

"So what is going to happen to Earth?" I demand.

"It will be scorched by four different kinds of radiation. It will be immediately uninhabitable."

"Un—" Mandy audibly gulps then tries again, "uninhabitable?"

"Yes," Baht nods, his glowing eyes the only movement inside that hood, "Radiation will immediately burn off half of Earth's ozone layer and ionize what is left of the atmosphere. Those that survive the initial catastrophe will no doubt die soon after from continuous nitrous-oxide inhalation coupled with lethel radiation—"

"Oh god! Wha—" She looks around wildly, "We need to fold immediately! Oh'Teck! Crystal and Brad! We need to get them!" She turns to me, "Your parents!"

I nod dumbly. Of course. We should get my parents.

A tentacle slides around my waist and I pat it absently.

"And—and others!" She wildly turns and grabs Seven's arms, "How many humans can we fit on this ship?"

"One Hundred and seventy two," Ken answers.

"I—" I clear my throat, "I'll start a list of –"

I can't finish.

How do we decide who to rescue? A hundred and seventy two out of billions? Should we just get kids? That would be the right thing wouldn't it?

"Oh'Teck can fold from his observatory." Ken reminds us.

"Okay, so let's message him to abduct as many humans as possible and get out of there," Mandy instructs. Ken moves to quickly do her bidding.

Mandy turns back to the com display, "You said ten days?"

"Yes."

"And then two more until it reaches Earth." She shakes Seven's arm, "How many times can we fold to Earth and back in twelve days?"

"Near a thousand times, but it will take longer to load and unload all the humans so—" he takes a breath then says with finality, "Twice a day."

"So twenty-four times a hundred and seventy—"

She whips around to look at the screen, "Baht—"

"I cannot help you."

"But—"

"I cannot."

And then he disconnects the com link from his end.

Well shit.